CA[...]
IN THE CRADLE

WILE E. YOUNG

NIGHT BLIGHT PRESS

This Edition Copyright © 2024 by Wile E. Young

Originally published in 2019 by Death's Head Press

The story included in this publication is a work of fiction. Any names or characters, businesses or places, events or incidents, are fictitious. Any resemblance to actual persons, living or dead, or actual events is purely coincidental.

Without limiting the rights under copyright reserved above, no part of this publication may be reproduced, stored in or introduced into a retrieval system, or transmitted, in any form, or by any means (electronic, mechanical, photocopying, recording, or otherwise), without the prior written permission of both the copyright owner and the above publisher of this book.

Cover Art by Anton Rosovsky

Map Art by BMR Williams

Cover Design & Interior Layout by Scott Cole
(www.13visions.com)

ALSO FROM WILE E. YOUNG

Shades of the Black Stone

The Magpie Coffin

The Perfectly Fine House
(co-written with Stephen Kozeniewski)

Clickers Never Die
(co-written with Stephen Kozeniewski)

Dust Bowl Children
(co-written with Emily Young)

The Southern Gentleman's Guide to Murder and Persuasion: Collected Short Fiction

Disasterpieces
(co-written with Wesley Southard)

For A Few Souls More

Borealis

COMING SOON

Man Up

It Came Out of The Sky

The Black Magpie Vs. Hematophages

For Your Love I'd Eat The Whole Wide World

For my grandfather, Roger Rice.

Black Lake
Clinton Lake
Grady Pope's Cabin
Carter Lake
First Church of Uncertain
Channel Marker 158
Devil's Elbow
River Bend Restaurant
Carter's Chute
Fish Net Gap
Government Ditch
Shady Glade Cafe
Town of Uncertain
Caddo Lake
Johnson's Ranch
N
W
E
S

INTRODUCTION

CATFISH IN THE CRADLE FELT like the culmination of a dream when it was accepted and after six years, I still look fondly on my first published novel. In the pages of this book are the memories of countless hours spent on Caddo Lake, and people long gone from Uncertain, Texas.

Even though I had been writing seriously for five years and had two trunk novels under my belt, *Catfish* still reads like a freshman effort. Are there things I would change? Absolutely! Have I decided to do so? Absolutely not.

And the reason for that is my feeling of debt to this humid and fishy tale. Without this initial success, I wouldn't have reached where I am now. How could I change it when most folks seemed to love this ode to bayou days?

So, I decided to not change a single word, but that doesn't mean I can't add some things. This new edition comes with a map that lists the important locations and is accurate for the real lake and its environs.

I ate many breakfasts with my grandfather at Shady Glade.

Not two months ago, I got gas at Johnson's Ranch.

I know Carter Lake, Government Ditch, Clinton Chute, and all the others like the back of my hand. I've seen the huge alligators, swam with snapping turtles, and even reeled in a catfish or two in my time.

That muddy water flows through my veins and through the pages of this book.

And the spirits of so many good people still live in the bayou's cypress moss, and if you ever find yourself on Caddo Lake, you'll see them too.

I can't wait to go back, just like I can't wait for all of you to return here to story of a man and his grandson, because in a place like Uncertain, Texas, blood does run thicker than water.

—WILE E. YOUNG, 2024

CHAPTER ONE

IT'S BEEN ABOUT A YEAR since my daughter went missing.

Stuff like that happens. You know it ain't all that rare; women just up and run off with whatever smooth talking man that's able to promise whatever makes their hearts flutter.

I had gotten the unwanted looks of sympathy, heard the hushed diner conversations… poor Grady Pope, his daughter done run off.

I pretended not to know, gave my own private misgivings to my friends and just prayed that whatever guy Sammie Jo had run off with was worth the humiliation her dear old dad had suffered.

"There you go hun, the Mr. Roger special just the way you like it."

I was snapped out of my stupor by the pretty little waitress that I would have jumped head over heels into to bed with in my younger years.

"Thanks Vicky."

Victoria Barnes was the talk of Uncertain, Texas. Even as she walked away, I could see the furtive glances from most of the men in the room trying to pretend they were drooling over their food.

Vicky had been good friends with Sammie Jo. Maybe that was why I was a little soft on her, with wishful thinking and alcohol attempting to form a replacement for my flesh and blood.

I dug into my pancakes and bacon with fervor; I had spent all night out on the lake looking for a particular gator that had been taking dogs and chickens near some lake houses. No kids yet thankfully, but once a gator started getting this bold it was only a matter of time before taxpayer was the only menu item.

Government work was shit, but it put the food on the table. Literally, since every animal I put down stocked my fridge for the next month. But nevertheless, it was a dirty job and I had often come home smelling to high heaven and coated in the insides of some critter or another. The pay wasn't fantastic, and if it weren't for the fact that the cabin had been in the family since my great-grandfather, I doubted I would have been able to afford it.

I was a simple man and content with it.

Sammie Jo had wanted more.

I sighed and rubbed my eyes, letting the warm egg yolk run down my throat as I stared around the Shady Glade Café, trying to keep my mind off my melancholy.

CATFISH IN THE CRADLE

The restaurant had been in business off and on for ninety years; people from all walks had traded yarns at the tables and stuffed their mouths with the finest food that the diner could provide. Battered chairs and checkerboard print tablecloths made up the interior of the place, walls of fishing gear and photos going back years all with smiling locals and secret spots known to select few.

The smell of breakfast food drifted from the pick-up window as Davis "Monster" Trucker deftly handled spatulas and deep fryers like he was a Hibachi chef down in Shreveport.

Sheriff Otis Porter was telling another anecdote to the regulars, fisherman, and others.

Mose William had a group of eager young tourists, no doubt guiding them through the canoe trails cut through the bayou.

Then there was Vicky, busy refilling Gideon Whyte's coffee, leaning over so the young fisherman could get a good look up her shirt. Best way to hook a man; appeal to his stomach and pecker simultaneously.

"Want a refill Grady?"

"Naw, I think I'm heading out."

Vicky leaned down and gave me a quick kiss on my unshaved cheek. "You take care you hear?"

I told her I would, gave her a generous tip and picked up my cap as I headed out the door. The chime rang as I stepped out into the gravel parking lot and breathed in a deep lungful of humid April air.

The marina was down a small mossy embankment to my left, and I strode purposefully out onto the dock past the ranks of Bass Masters, Sun Trackers, and aluminum bottom River Runners. Most folks around here paid for their own slips, but I just tied up at the very end of the row, right past the last slip on the open water.

My pride and joy was a Lowe 175 that I had saved and scraped to buy. I loosed the moorings and pushed off the dock, pontoons under the wood bouncing in the water as I pulled away. The engine rumbled to life and I motored out into the channel, lily pads and Spanish moss bouncing in my wake.

I could smell the muddy water from the river and reached my hand over, letting the water gently stroke my fingers as a startled turtle jumped into the water from a nearby log.

Caddo Lake was a little over 25,000 acres of wetland and lake in deep East Texas, the Louisiana border a hot stone's throw away. Cypress trees enshrouded the area... a place to come if you wanted to disappear from the world.

I glanced at the empty seat next to the trolling motor on the prow of my boat and the melancholy came drifting back. Just as well; this wasn't the place to come if you wanted the high life. I made my way up river in silence hearing the occasional quack of a duck or a distant crow, lost in my own thoughts.

My home was located in a back channel dominated by small inlets and trees called Carter Lake, very far off the beaten path, which was just the way that I liked it. I rounded the corner in the bend and saw the squat dull-brown wood and faded windows of my humble cabin, a craggy slope dominated by dead driftwood and cypress trees obscuring the view.

Then I heard the sobbing.

The water down by my boathouse was shallow and muddy. I had grown used to the various blacks, greens, and dull greys of the things that grew and drifted there.

So the pale flesh huddled under one of the support beams threw me for a loop.

I gunned the motor faster and hollered over the lapping waves "Hello! You okay?"

A face peeked out at me: long blonde hair covered in mud, tear-stained eyes misted over in drops of agony, long red scrapes from where the woods had torn at the flesh.

My daughter... Sammie Jo screamed under the dock, her massively swollen belly heaving in the throes of labor.

CHAPTER TWO

THERE'S NO CELLPHONE RECEPTION OUT in the boonies, one of the side effects of living in the sticks. I had seen full-grown men lose their shit and throw tantrums once they were disconnected from the wider world. That was the thing about Uncertain and Caddo Lake… if you needed to get lost, you just needed to take a walk into the bayou.

The clay-like mud splattered all over my jeans and flannel shirt as I crouched in the muck with my daughter.

"*Sammie!*" I was practically sobbing as I scooped her up in my arms. Her eyes, which had been wrinkled in tears and pain, softened for a moment before she gritted her teeth and let loose another ear-splitting shriek.

It wasn't like delivering puppies. I had done that plenty of times. But a real baby was outside my expertise.

I tried to pick her up but my old bones weren't up to the task, and I barely managed to get her out of the muck and filth and onto the dock. The wood was warm from having baked under the sun, its soft rays trying to reach down and provide a little comfort before it turned the world into an oven.

I blinked into the light and mouthed the words *Please God* over and over as my daughter shrieked, her belly quivering.

Her mother had given birth to her in Shreveport at Promise Hospital. It had been a surprise labor. I had been out on the river and our neighbor Cy had to drive Renee into town. The nurses had given me death glares when I had tracked mud into the ward, telling me to leave, but I had managed to muscle pass just in time to see my beautiful baby girl, born seven pounds and four ounces in the cool autumn of 1986.

I rocked Sammie Jo in my arms. "Push on through baby girl, push on through... I know it hurts."

There weren't any neighbors coming to help me. Cy had passed ten years ago, and no one wanted to buy a cabin nearly five miles from the nearest road with no reception. I kept praying for a miracle, that maybe Scott Carter or one of my other friends would come trundling up the driveway to check on me.

Sammie shrieked again and her nails, chipped and dirty, dug into my arms, drawing dark maroon blood that trickled down my forearm and onto her breasts and chest.

I wished for Renee. She would have known what to do... she had taken all those classes about it while I just had a very simple knowledge. But my wife had passed too, six months ago. Sammie Jo disappearing had aged her overnight.

"Baby girl, I can see the head!"

I didn't know if it was a boy or girl, but a head of pallid black hair was showing, then another contraction, and another push... a face.

Sammie caterwauled and shouted cuss words to high heaven, her pain intense as I gripped her hand and told her what a good job she was doing. That's what I had seen in the movies... there wasn't much else I could do.

A final scream and a push and my grandson spilled out onto the dock, crying his lungs out. Sammie Jo fell back with a groan, and I hastily took off my jacket and scooped the boy up into my arms, trying to keep him warm.

The boy's cries were deep, more croak than wailing, throaty... I hadn't remembered his mother making such noise. His hands grasped at the air, brushing the strands from my beard as he experienced the world for the first time.

I smiled "Baby girl, it's a boy..." Sammie Jo didn't respond, and my smile disappeared and a heavy pressure grappled with my heart. I set the boy down gently in my coat and shook Sammie's shoulders. "Baby girl..."

Her eyes were dilated and were staring sightlessly out at the bayou. I shook her shoulders harder, her head bouncing on the dock like a fish out of water.

I screamed her name over and over again, her child joining in the symphony of pain as the sun burned my bare skin, uncaring.

Her hair was spread out like ripples in water, her eyes and mouth a painting of relief.

She was dead.

I rocked back and forth, begging her to come back, the stabbing pain in my heart unending.

The boy squirming in my jacket caught my eye; the little thing could barely move as he grasped at the air… unaware that his mother was gone.

My old bones creaked when I stood; I stood over the thing that had killed my daughter. Those eyes that weren't open yet, mouth that opened and closed repeatedly, the pale skin that still glistened with the juices of childbirth.

He was a murderer, a killer. My daughter's corpse lay feet away, the death wound between her legs all the evidence I needed.

All I had to do was nudge him off the dock, let him sink into the brown water, his first taste of life nothing but an illusion.

It would be justice.

The temptation was there to my shame; my grandson barely into the world and already with an enemy.

I could have done it easily, I owed him no loyalty. No loyalty other than blood, thicker than the water lapping at the bank.

I picked him up cradling him gently and I walked to my truck, turning on the heater and driving into town.

Lincoln, that's what I named him. Lincoln Andrew Pope, my first and only grandchild.

Marshall, Texas was about a fifteen-minute drive from Uncertain. I thundered down the highway, ignoring any speed limit signs until I had reached the Christus Good Shepherd Medical Center.

A nurse had made a small noise of alarm when I had come stumbling through the door, all sweat and dirt carrying a squalling baby. Lincoln was practically wrenched from my hands and taken into the depths of the hospital as clipboards full of forms were shoved in my hands.

My handwriting was sloppy; the little one room schoolhouse in Karnack having done little to equip me with any useful skills. I hadn't graduated and could barely add and subtract. I had spent my childhood outdoors on the lake under my father's guidance and stories.

The paper was a mess of scribbles, and for the first time I wondered who the father was. As she had gotten, older Sammie Jo had spent time enough trawling bars for men… I had never met any of them. That was the one bit of mercy my daughter had left me: a blessed ignorance of how she spent time away from home.

There would be tests, maybe a DNA test, to prove he was kin, an end to mystery.

Then I would know the identity of the man who had taken my little girl.

The police came walking in like they owned the place, typical East Texas swagger… this wasn't Otis Porter and his deputies; these were city police.

I repeated the story of my daughter's disappearance that every mouth in Uncertain could have repeated verbatim and told them to call anyone to back me up.

They kept pushing, asking hard questions and trying to press my buttons. I was a man with a temper, but I wasn't rising to the occasion. If I did there was no hope for Lincoln... he'd grow up without a mother or grandfather. The Popes are a stubborn clan, always have been and always will be... lasting through the tides and the seasons.

Otis was finally called. He vouched for me and I was free to leave.

Lincoln had to stay at the hospital; he needed more than I could give him, not to mention the tests to prove his blood relation to me. They at least let me see him first.

The nursery had that odd sterile smell that had always made me uncomfortable. My mother had died in a rest home, and every time I had gone to visit her towards the end that stench had left with me, lingering all the way back to the house.

Lincoln was front and center, dressed in that little blue outfit that hospitals kept on hand for baby boys. He wriggled and squirmed, and for the first time I was struck by how pallid his skin was... unhealthy, like he had never seen a sun before.

Then it was time to leave, and I was in my truck driving back to Uncertain.

My adrenaline died.

And my grief began.

CHAPTER THREE

I PULLED OVER ON THE edge of the road between Marshall and Uncertain. I had driven past this spot a million times and could have probably pointed out every rabbit hole or possum den for miles. The pasture to the left, the overhanging tree, the mud stained boulder that had seen too many rainstorms.

I pounded the steering wheel, shouting out my anguish and letting the tears fall. If you cry, always do it away from prying eyes. My father had pounded that lesson into me at the end of a fist. One too many black eyes and pain began to lose its potency.

But I had never felt pain like this.

When I had finished, I wiped my face and focused on that dead pit in my stomach, the one I went to when things were bad.

The one that made me angry.

Sheriff Otis Porter and his deputy Beau were waiting when I got back to the cabin. Their old cruiser had seen better days; a holdover from the eighties, it still had the swiveling lights instead of the strobe lights of more modern cars. It was parked right next to the door with a black van that belonged to my friend Scott Carter.

I turned off the ignition and climbed out. Otis waited for me patiently next to the house. An overweight man in his fifties, he had been a star high school quarterback in his day. He still looked capable, though, even if he was packing a bit of a spare tire.

"Grady..." We shook hands, his eyes echoing his sympathy without words. Southern upbringing all the way: never voice the problem. "Scott's already down at the dock."

I nodded and gruffly murmured a thanks before the three of us walked around the house and down the embankment to my boat slip. They had pulled a sheet over her body, a blessing and a mercy.

Scott walked to meet us and hugged me in a short embrace. "Grady."

"Thanks for coming Scott."

My friend nodded, his goatee that was just beginning to show hints of grey contrasting with the dark navy t-shirt he was wearing. "We are gonna take her into Marshall if you'll let us, get an autopsy."

They wanted to cut my baby girl up, tear her open with no dignity for a cause of death that I already knew...

CATFISH IN THE CRADLE

"That'll be fine, but I want a DNA test done on the kid, find out who the father is and if he's going to be a problem."

Otis and Beau nodded and promised they'd get the order put through. None of us said the word *rape*, but it was obvious that it was going through our minds. And if it was true…

Well, folks around here have a way of dealing with that.

My boat had drifted into a small grove of cypress trees, and Beau slipped on an extra pair of waders to retrieve it. I walked with Scott and Otis as they gathered up Sammie Jo, carrying her as gently as two middle aged men could up the hill. They gently placed her in the back of the van, sealing her in the body bag that had been brought for her.

There was my daughter, seemingly at peace. But I had seen that look of fear in her eyes before Lincoln had made his way into the world. She hadn't been at peace then.

She had been afraid.

"You uh, you gonna be okay?" Otis Porter wasn't very good at comforting words. His true forte was in profanity, and when the boys gathered down at Johnson's Ranch for game night he was hurling four-letter words like they were on clearance.

I nodded. Otis and Scott both promised they would treat her with the utmost respect and decency and that they would send for me when they had news. Most of their words were a haze lost in the late morning heat.

Beau reappeared his boots caked with mud and with a few fresh mosquito bites. He climbed in the cruiser followed by Otis. Their wheels kicked up dust as they left, Scott's van following in their wake.

I wanted to reach out. Whether my daughter was in the back of that van and dead or not, I didn't want her to go.

The engine sounds followed long after the cypress woods had swallowed them, and I listened until that was only a memory replaced with distant crows, chattering.

I shuffled and looked up at the sun and its merciless gaze, and then I slowly shambled my way back into the cabin. The whole building was single story, low roof, and wood and brick that generations of blood and sweat had maintained. Four bedrooms: one for Renee and I, two for the kids we had intended to have that had ended up only being one, and another for guests. Renee had been ecstatic when I had replaced the ancient carpet with wood, polished oak floors that had felt weird to walk across at first, especially in the winter when I was used to the carpet warming my old feet.

The silence wasn't new. I had been living with it for a year.

There was tiny part of me past the bitterness that hoped Lincoln would bring life back into this place, that the boy would grow up here in the bayou learning the ins and outs like his mother had, that he could find the joy in it that had eluded her.

The old red easy chair was a relic from a previous decade; Renee had always hated that chair and begged me to let her buy me a new one. But through tide, time, and my stubbornness, the chair had stayed. A small table stained with round circles from years of condensation on cups and glass sat next to the chair. A few old family photos were arrayed across it.

CATFISH IN THE CRADLE

I reached for the nearest one and looked at my wife, as beautiful thirty years ago as when she took her last breath, Sammie Jo just a baby in her arms like Lincoln was in the nursery right now.

The weariness set in and I leaned back in the chair, staring at the picture as I sobbed myself into a dreamless sleep.

It was a low sound that woke me, a deep vibration in my chest like a train churning across a distant railroad.

I had heard a fog horn before, but it didn't sound like that. It sounded rougher, like the inside of whatever was being blown caught the sound to deform the note. It was close, outside my cabin; I blinked my eyes and stared at the light coming through the window.

It was late afternoon; the sun had settled behind the cypress trees and turned the world into a tapestry of long shadows and islands of fading light. The light in the cabin was dim, but a hunter's instinct had seized me.

I wasn't alone.

The gun cabinet was across the room and took only seconds to open. The .308 hunting rifle was like an old friend in my hands.

The horn sounded again.

I eased out the back door, making my way around the house towards the tree line and the sound. All kinds of mischief haunted these woods and possibilities flitted through my mind, childhood fears come back to life.

Everyone in Uncertain had grown up hearing tall tales about the Robichaudes, a family who lived deep in the bayou. Rumor had it that they practiced all sorts of witchcraft. I couldn't speak to black magic, but the fact of the matter was that people who harassed them usually met with some ill fate not long after. Supposedly... hearsay and belief ruled around here much more than fact.

Maybe that was why the lynch mob had hung them from the rafters of their own home.

The Robichaudes had lived not too far from me, on the back lake, when I had heard the noise I had gone to investigate.

I still remembered that trek through the bayou; hadn't stopped when the branches cut my skin or when I had twisted my ankle on an outstretched root. All of that and I had still been too late. Their murderers had come and gone, leaving only a little boy screaming at the sight of his kin's bodies.

It was a town secret, and no one had stepped forward all those years ago to claim responsibility. I had my suspicions but no proof... Still I had seen the guilty faces on Sunday mornings in church. There was no disguising shame.

To this day I could still hear those faint screams.

With no phone it had been up to me, and I had arrived in time to find the bodies.

There weren't any dead Cajuns out to haunt me for my failures today. Just some assholes eager to catch a bullet.

It might have been the Klan; sheet-wearing bastards had been a thorn around this town for years. Thoughts of meth heads looking for a new place to cook drifted through my mind.

CATFISH IN THE CRADLE

A quick glance at Cy's vacant cabin confirmed that it was still empty.

Teenage idiots looking to see where someone had actually died then...

The Spanish moss hid me, and my wide boots were quiet on the leaves. As I crept through the woods, I briefly worried about coming up on a snake before I decided that it didn't really matter.

Grief does crazy things to the mind.

The horn blew another time, down by the boat slip. I couldn't see anyone there at least not out in the backyard that the sun still held dominion over.

Whoever was down there was standing in the shadow of the boathouse where the reflections in the water played tricks the eye. I thought I could see someone squatting close by the water. At least I thought it was someone; the shadows and the onset of night were playing hell with my vision.

I crept though the woods until I was close. Then I sprinted from the woods, screaming hellfire and thunder, squeezing off a shot into the sky. That had always worked in the past when trespassers or hunters a little too far off their leases wandered onto the property.

I expected to hear some screaming and a few teenagers go running, but instead there was nothing but silence and the breeze blowing through the trees.

I walked up to the boathouse. The slip was undisturbed my Lowe resting serenely in its moorings. No one was standing on the dock. My eyes were drawn to the spot where Sammie Jo had gasped her last and brought my grandson into the world only hours before. It felt like a different life. The smell still lingered; I had forgotten to clean it up, and Scott had been more concerned with making sure my daughter's body was properly cared for.

There was wetness around the spot, like someone dripping water had been standing there only moments before.

I looked around, peering inside the boathouse for anyone hiding in the shadows. I clicked on the light; the small dingy bulb coated in a small layer of dust cast its feeble orange light around the boathouse. The inside was really just a small wooden platform that had just enough room for a small workbench and a wall full of rods, reels, and tackle.

I made sure that the winch and pulleys for my boat hadn't been tampered with and that no one was hiding inside it before I walked back outside.

There was no one there.

I slumped against one of the support pillars keeping the boathouse from sinking down into the muck of the river. This was senility, or dementia, Alzheimer's and whatever else affected the elderly... my hands weren't as strong as they used to be, and my eyes were shot to shit.

Age was creeping in.

Good riddance.

Maybe it was instinct or maybe it was because it was the only noise other than my ragged breathing, but my gaze was drawn to the river. It was floating there right below the dock where I was, circular, like a Christmas wreath but made of black driftwood. It was decorated with wilted yellow

CATFISH IN THE CRADLE

dogwoods, black grassy moss, and lily pad shavings that were already beginning to droop as life left them.

I jumped off the dock, my knees popping as they hit the shallow water and mud. I picked the object up into my hands, the flowers and decorations falling off into the water.

The circular driftwood had something carved in it, words or symbols that I couldn't read.

Still, it was proof that someone had been here.

I suddenly felt watched. But there was no one in the trees, no one sitting in a boat in the water, nothing but me and the wreath held in my hand.

I turned to walk back up to the cabin, snatching my rifle from the dock.

One more thing caught my eye as the sun went down; I squinted against the encroaching night and could barely make out the outline of a footprint next to the bank. I knew it wasn't my own, but the light and my failing vision must have been playing hell with me.

Every toe looked like it had been connected.

CHAPTER FOUR

I WENT TO SHADY GLADE the next morning like I had always done.

I had fallen asleep on my chair; rifle resting across my lap and wet idol on the couch side table. It was currently resting on the passenger seat next to me, no less strange in the light of day. I had spent the rest of the previous evening on guard hoping, praying, and worrying that whoever had left this thing would return.

They never did.

It was a bright day. The mosquitoes were buzzing as I made my way down the channel and out in the main river. There weren't many boats on the river this morning, though I knew that it was because the world hadn't woken up and got to shaking itself free of the morning dew that had accumulated throughout the night. By midday this place would be choked with party barges and speedboats filled with folks eager to get away from real life for a while and lose themselves in the booze and the river of mud.

I sighed and rubbed a hand through my grey hair as I took the Devil's Elbow turnaround and entered Government Ditch. From there it was just a short jaunt to the Shady Glade marina.

There was a pause in conversation when that chime above the door rang and people saw just who it was that was walking in.

Little known fact about small towns: there isn't anything to talk about until something big happens. Sammie Jo was one of those bits of gossip that would have spread around like wild fire; at least three tables in this place had probably been talking about her when I walked through the damn door.

I found an empty table in the back right corner right next to the window and waited for Vicky to bring me my morning coffee. She sauntered over with a steaming pot clutched in her hand. She put a hesitant hand on my shoulder, her eyes soft. "Grady we heard… I'm so sorry."

I nodded my head and gave some gruff words of thanks; I wasn't well equipped for accepting pity or sorrow. I had been raised under the philosophy to never let them see you bleed. I was prepared for round after round of this treatment for the rest of the day. I expected a few sympathy pies, maybe even a visit from Pastor Arnold and his wife, offering me the church's deepest condolences.

It was all bullshit.

Not that the sympathy, the pity, and the comfort wasn't real, but it would be over just as quick. I'd become nothing

CATFISH IN THE CRADLE

more than Old Man Pope living out in the woods with his grandson whose mama ran off then came back and died. Everything would be swept under the rug and forgotten except for warning stories for little girls to listen to their daddies.

Vicky brought me my traditional food and I tried to stomach every morsel that usually brought me satisfaction but now turned to ashes in my stomach. Sorrow has a way of discoloring everyday life, especially when the wound is fresh.

Davis Trucker heaved his bulk into the seat across from me, grease-stained white shirt straining to hold in his belly as wiped his sweaty brow with a napkin. "Congratulations and condolences, I suppose…"

Shady Glade's proprietor was a bombastic showman to his customers and a gruff man of few words to his friends; it was shocking when the mask came off to reveal who he really was. Davis had been everywhere and seen everything with a career that included ice road trucking, canoe guide, accountant… it was a common joke around the dives and eateries of Uncertain that you couldn't do anything that Davis Trucker had not already done before.

"So when do we get to see the little tyke?"

I didn't laugh or share in his small smile; the reality of the fact that I had a grandson hadn't sunk in yet. "When you drive your happy ass up to the hospital, though you couldn't make it through the door I expect."

Davis thumped his fingers lightly on the table as I took another bite of tasteless pancake. "Fat jokes. Thought we were long past that."

"We've never been past it, Davis." I grunted as I finished off the food.

"The boy is going to need some mothering. No offense to you Grady, but Renee was always the one with the better head on her shoulders."

I didn't bother trying to dispute that bit of wisdom. I was useful for practical skills, but nurturing social skills and emotional baggage was beyond me. Left to me, the boy would be able to survive in the wild and also be maladjusted to anywhere that was more concrete than wood.

"Folks have been talking, a few even considering helping out… that is if you'll let them into that old shack of yours."

I met Davis' eyes, his receding hairline doing nothing to hide the wrinkles that furrowed along his brow and caused him to look older than he actually was. He may have been quiet and thoughtful when around those in the know, but I had wondered over the years how much of the fun-loving boastful mask was fueled by secret desire.

Everyone wants to be someone different on occasion.

"How much I owe you for the food?"

Davis shook his head slowly and rose out of the chair. "It's on the house for today. You take care now Grady… bring the little fella by when he gets out of the hospital."

I didn't promise I would, but it didn't need to be said. It was considered a slap in the face of everyone if you didn't show off your new kin once they were ready.

Lincoln, alone in the hospital, filtered through my mind and I rose from my table making my way out to the dingy old payphone that Davis insisted on keeping. I slipped in fifty cents and listened for the dulcet sound of the dial tone before dialing Otis' number. He answered on the third ring.

"Yeah Otis, its Grady... I need a ride."

I grabbed the driftwood from my boat before Otis came trundling into Shady Glade's parking lot. The humidity and sun was already getting to the man as he waved at me and opened the door.

"What's that? Some kind of half-assed life preserver?"

I explained what had happened last night, the horn, the footprint... Otis snapped out of jackass mode and became the Sheriff as he started grilling me for details, questioning every little thing in hopes that there was something that had slipped my mind.

"What do you make of it?"

Otis shrugged, his eyes hard orbs that didn't betray his thoughts. "Honestly, that thing could be some old Indian shit or who knows... think you're stretching looking for some deeper meaning for Sammie's—" He cut himself off, not wanting to rip fresh scars. "Just think you're reaching is all."

Normally I would have agreed with him, but there was something nagging the back of my mind. Instinct or paranoia maybe, but regardless, there was a mental itch that I just couldn't scratch.

This shit wasn't normal.

I stifled my misgivings. Otis wasn't known for his patience when it came to things that he considered settled.

We talked sparingly for the rest of the drive into Marshall, mostly about the salvinia weed overtaking the lake, an anecdote about a drunk boater, the best fishing holes that we were sure only us alone knew about. Standard friendship chatter that didn't have much deeper meaning to it, easy talk that could have been discussed anywhere. The issue of Sammie Jo and Lincoln was not discussed at all.

We parked at the far side of the hospital lot and walked through the double doors, making our way to the nursery. Lincoln wasn't there. There were other boys and girls, but my grandson was nowhere to be seen.

A nurse appeared a second later. "Mr. Pope?" I nodded my mouth dry. "Will you please come with me? Dr. Riggs needs to talk to you."

"What's wrong with my grandson?" I asked immediately, my heart pumping, fear that there had been some unforeseen complication and he was now lying dead in the morgue.

"Lincoln is fine, Mr. Pope. The doctor just wants to talk to you about some of the things you'll be facing raising him."

I thought it was odd considering it was clear that I had already raised his mother, but I didn't complain as I left Otis in the waiting room to see Dr. Riggs.

The nurse was a liar.

Lincoln lay in a small crib, pretty standard for a hospital with its clear sides and blue blankets allowing easy viewing of the kicking boy. *Syndactyly* was what the doctor was calling it, fancy medical school word for the fact that my grandson had been born with webbed fingers and toes. They claimed it was nothing but fused skin and while it was rare that it wasn't life threatening, sour news for a man whose daughter had given birth to a kid that would have been at home in a freak show under the stage name Frog Boy.

Then there were the birth defects on his neck, scars that had been formed in the womb, lines that would mark him the rest of his life.

I knew I was being harsh. The boy hadn't chosen to become like this, and the part of me that was rational and loyal to blood knew that I would care for the kid. That darker side though, the one that I kept under lock and key but close to the surface, looked down at Lincoln with disgust, to my everlasting shame.

"Mr. Pope, do you have all that?"

Dr. Riggs was a bookish man well into his forties who looked like his personal moment of educational pride was being the teacher's pet. He had talked slowly, enunciating every few words just to be sure that I understood exactly what he was talking about.

It was true that a majority of it flew right over my head, but the man's lack of respect was already grating at my temper and I was fighting back the rage I felt twisting around my bones.

"Yeah, I got it doc. When can I take the boy?"

Riggs looked taken aback. Probably wasn't used to someone disregarding his authority so easily, and when he spoke again his voice was lower.

"Well uh, I think we can discharge him today. Judge Dowd already signed custody over to you in lieu of a will as his closest living relative."

I licked my lips. "What about the DNA test I want?"

Riggs shook his head. "Chief Wiley is running that one… you'll have to talk to him.'"

After that it was a questionnaire about proper child care, like I hadn't changed hundreds of diapers before. But eventually I was released out into a waiting room while the nurses prepped Lincoln for his first journey into the outside world.

A nurse with red hair that I would have flirted with as a younger man brought him out. She cooed over him, smiling at me as she handed the boy over. "He's strong, sir!'

She was chipper, and I did my best to return the smile as I firmly cradled the boy close to the chest. Those big round black eyes stared up at me and a little hand grasped at the air, webbed fingers causing my insides to turn flips in revulsion as I carried him out of the waiting room and into the world.

We stopped and bought a car seat. Strapping the boy tightly in the back seat, Otis' eyes had widened when he had seen Lincoln's condition, but he chose not to comment. Maybe he should have since the ride back to Uncertain was filled with a quiet tension that I was unused to around my friend.

I broke the silence. "They said that skin grafts were an option but I don't have that kind of money…"

Otis didn't let his eyes leave the road. "He's in for a hard road. You know how kids are."

I sure did. Back in my little one room schoolhouse with a class of twenty there had always been someone to pick on. I could already see my grandson's destiny written large across the cypress moss and small-town prejudice.

Freak.

"It'll toughen him up. We came through it okay, right?" Otis said.

I chuckled. "It's been a long time since I had any hint of schooling, Otis. Back then you had to be tough if you just wanted to survive recess."

The Sheriff smiled, his eyes traveling back to distant memories that only he knew. "Yeah. I hear you. Back in my day if you shot out another kid's eye with a pellet gun you had to give him a free pack of BBs to make up for it."

We both smiled at the shared nostalgia. Hell, compared to today, our childhoods were practically barbaric. But it had also seemed more innocent… no iPods, cellphones, or weird toys that had no useful purpose.

That was the time I had met Renee, hair shining bright on the jungle gym as she hung upside down, staring hard at the sun. I had turned to old Delton Robby, long since passed away, and said, "That's the girl I'm going to marry…"

I was a man of my word through and through.

Lincoln's braying brought me out of my memory and I twisted around in my seat to look at him. "It's alright kid, your Pop is gonna take good care of you… not going to let anything hurt you."

Sometimes I wonder if it would have been better had we left him on the side of the road that day.

CHAPTER FIVE

I TOOK THE RIDE HOME slow; Lincoln had calmed down as soon as I had set him on the passenger seat of my boat, his caterwauling dwindling away to a pleased coo and eventually sleep.

I barely kept the motor running, making sure that the sounds of the engine were a light puttering instead of a mighty roar, going even slower when a boat full of tourists thundered past. The 175 bobbed over each wake. I didn't want to risk waking the boy by jumping the waves, and even with the calm rocking I was afraid that Lincoln would wake up and begin his screaming again.

He kept right on sleeping, oblivious to the roiling river.

I took the turn off the main river and into the back channels leading to Carter's Lake. The noise died away except for the sound of the engine sputtering and the secret world enshrouded by the cypress trees. I heard a distant hiss and a fearful bleating as an alligator made lunch out of a wild goat or deer that had wandered too close to the water; I wondered if it was the same one that I had been contracted to remove…

I glanced at Lincoln; a job that was going to get infinitely harder now that I had a young'un to look after.

We were almost back when the woods went quiet. A lifetime in the outdoors had taught me that when the world fell silent you had best be ready to fight for your life.

I killed the engine and let the current take us down the channel while I unclasped the panel that opened into the hull. I pulled a small lock box that contained my Model 29 revolver, a small case of .44 magnum cartridges sitting beside it. I quickly loaded the weapon and began scanning the water.

It was rare that an alligator would attack a boat, especially one the size of mine. But I had been wrong before. The scratches and teeth marks in the boat's paint from a sixteen-foot monster were still unrepaired to this day. Fisherman told tales of bigger ones, and in this part of the lake I wouldn't have doubted that one would have found a home.

The water was eerily still, the current disappearing and leaving Lincoln and I drifting on dead water. This area was more swamp than river, a narrow channel and shallow water flooded with green lily pads and cloistering trees drowning the place in shadows. Predators lurked here. I had once seen a cougar prowling the shore… the lack of human activity let the animals pursue their instincts without fear.

I heard a thump behind me and the boat turned to the left. I stumbled and instinctively reached out to grab the car seat.

That feeling of being watched that I had experienced the previous evening returned, and I glanced around the marshy bog, eyes traveling over every nook and branch looking for a camouflaged hunter or a boat hidden by logs… anything indicating a human presence.

Maybe it was the fact that the birds had gone quiet, or maybe it was because it sounded unnatural. Either way I heard a sound that I couldn't immediately identify, but then a lifetime of stepping out of a shower or bathtub reminded me that I had heard that noise all too often.

It was the sound of dripping water.

You wouldn't think that the sound of water would be out of place in a swamp, but when you were dealing with mostly dead water in a bog the sound was alien. It was echoing from a dense cluster of cypress trees that huddled close. Even in the bright sun I couldn't make out if anything was there.

"Whoever's back there you better come on out now unless you want a hole in your gut."

Nothing moved.

That sound of dripping water was starting to die away but I could still barely hear it. Whoever was standing in that grove of trees must have been wearing the best camouflage in the world…

Obscured by trees or not, a man can't hide from fear.

I pointed the pistol a little ways off towards a lily pad and pulled the trigger. The lily pad exploded as the calm day was split by the resounding *crack* and smell of gunpowder. Birds took off in panic from the trees, but nothing moved in that small grove of cypress.

The sound was gone.

Lincoln had woken with the gunshot and his squalling had begun anew. I carefully unloaded the gun before leaning down and rocking the car seat, shushing him. "It's okay, my boy, it's okay. Just a gator trying to get a meal…" Even the words rang hollow on my tongue as I glanced back at the cypress trees in the middle of the bog.

With my grandson awake I didn't bother trying to putter around. I clambered back into the driver's seat and kicked on the engine. The machine roared to life and I gunned the throttle, rocketing away from the bog.

Otis had apparently called everyone to let them know I was bringing Lincoln home. Too many cars were waiting in the driveway to my liking, and a small crowd was gathered on the grass slope that led up to my house. They began clapping when they saw my boat round the corner into the small bayou, Scott Carter and Davis Trucker among them.

Truth be told I was uncomfortable with the attention. Probably why I preferred the solitude of the sticks versus a pretty house in town.

Scott and Davis helped me tied up the boat while Vicky whisked Lincoln out of the passenger seat. The boy was still mewling, and I was secretly grateful that I didn't have him right beside my ear, crying at full blast for the time being.

The two Game Wardens, Larry Knowles and Desmond Miles, stood just behind them.

"Congratulations, old man!" Larry hollered.

I smiled in return, trying not to recall all of the tickets they had given me over the years. Larry Knowles was a man in his early thirties, one of those who had peaked early in his career and was now stuck in his job until he retired with a beer gut and years worth of stories. At the moment he had managed to keep himself in fairly good shape, though his five o'clock shadow had turned into a seven o'clock beard.

Desmond Miles on the other hand didn't speak much of his past, but from the rumors and hearsay around Uncertain it was quite the tale, one that no one exactly knew other than his pretty wife, Susannah, and she wasn't talking either. Heard the Klan had tried to make him a victim and hadn't walked out of the bayou alive to tell of it. Never found any bodies, but if I were a betting man they had graced some lucky alligator's gullet.

"Thanks for coming," I said gruffly wishing Renee was there; she'd always been the people person.

Earl Ray and his wife Sue had come up from down the road. A hard man with rippling muscles and a Bud Light clutched in his hand, Otis had handed him more DWIs than greetings over the years. Sue was a quiet woman in a blue sundress and looked like she had just hit thirty despite being a good decade older. Her blonde hair shimmered under the summer sun as her eyes fell over my grandson and she cooed reaching in to grab his tiny hand.

Davis' wife Maggie embraced me as I exited the boathouse "He's going to be real handsome, like his grandpa."

"Hopefully his other one." I replied gruffly.

"They get any results on that DNA test?" Earl Ray asked as he wandered up, his grey goatee stained with tobacco juice.

"Otis didn't say anything about it other than he'd let me know when the city police got the results back."

That devolved into a long swirling argument about how the cops didn't think too highly of the low-income backwoods folk like us that I half listened to. My thoughts were still with Sammie Jo.

Maybe they could tell despite my attempts to hide my emotion, but I found Gideon Whyte shoving a beer into my hand and clicking the can "To Sammie Jo…"

The cry was repeated by everyone who had a drink in hand as we bottomed up under the sun. My grandson's homecoming had become a makeshift wake.

No one got wasted on beer. That would have been bad taste at something like this… just sips and reminiscing on old times and speculating about Lincoln and his future.

Likewise no one commented on the boy's webbed hands and feet. Just like no one commented when a baby was born around here with a different skin color than the father, folks would much rather avoid the subject that point out the obvious.

They say it takes a community, and my neighbors had obliged. Otis had given me the car seat, Vicky and Gideon had bought a mess of baby formula, Earl Ray and Sue some hand me down baby clothes, Davis and Maggie a few toys… All of it I was most grateful for since I hadn't been planning on raising a child yesterday.

They promised to stop by more often and help out if they could. They knew my job and they knew how much time it consumed along with the dangers that came with it. Lincoln wouldn't be joining me in the hunt until he was much older.

Vicki had the day off tomorrow, and she promised that she and Gideon would come over to watch Lincoln in the morning so I could hunt. I gave them my thanks and they left along with Earl Ray, Sue, and the Truckers.

Only Scott Carter was left, though he looked like he would rather be anywhere else than on my property. I knew that it was something to do with Sammie Jo, but I didn't want to voice it. Instead we shot the breeze about the current baseball season and if the Saints were going to go all the way this year, Lincoln oblivious in his car seat next to me, tired from the day's events.

Scott laughed from a joke I had made, but the merriment disappeared from his face and was replaced by a morose reluctance. "Grady, there's uh… well… I started the autopsy and found some—" He paused, searching for the right words. "Some surprising facts that you might not want to hear about, especially when it comes to your daughter, but I—"

I interrupted him. "Scott, no offense, but would you hurry the hell up and just tell me what you found?"

Scott nodded and licked his lips. "Well, her uh… genitals were mutilated by the birth, but I found large traces of mercury in her blood…"

I shook my head, lost to what my friend was saying. "You saying that she ate a thermometer or something?"

Scott shook his head. "She would have had to eat a lot of thermometers. More likely someone poisoned her…"

Murder… it had been murder…

I knew it.

"Hopefully the DNA test can reveal more, but this whole situation is looking less like an accident."

I didn't react or respond. No use letting Scott know that if I found the name of the philandering son of a bitch who had killed my baby girl I would put a bullet between his eyes.

"I'm going to give Otis the results when I get back into town, looking more than likely this is criminal…"

I nodded my head, eyes hard as I looked down at Lincoln. If they hadn't already cleared him at the hospital I would have been running to my truck to take him back. But instead he was happy and healthy but for his condition.

"I have to get going, but you take care now you hear?" I told Scott that I would, told him to watch for deer and went back into my house before the dust had settled.

I was going to have to redo Sammie Jo's room. We had only ever had one guest room and Renee wouldn't have stood by and let me tear it apart so I could keep my shrine to our daughter intact.

Her room wasn't overly big:, a bed in the middle with brown sheets and a mess of decorative pillows on the headboard, objects with no point or purpose in my opinion. Her dresser was on the wall that ran along the edge of the house, under the window. The sunlight filtering through blinds washed over my baby girl's bright and smiling face in a march of picture frames from when she was a child all the way to a grown woman.

Renee and I hadn't sent her to Karnack, preferring to let her get a proper education at the bigger school in Marshall. Sammie Jo had been full of life, participated in athletics, made the cheerleading squad, and had the guys chasing after her... a quality she must have gotten from her mother.

I felt the tears welling in my eyes again as I began to take down the pictures, wracking sobs spiraled across my chest as I pulled cardboard boxes out of the attic and began unpacking her dresser, the clothes from her closet fitting tightly together. Memorabilia, toys, ancient knick knacks that she had acquired over her twenty-eight years of life disappeared into the depths of the cardboard, most likely to never see the light of day ever again.

Not for the first time I regretted being unable to afford Sammie's wish to go to college. It wasn't like she had even wanted to go very far away. East Texas Baptist University was located right there in Marshall. We wouldn't have had to pay for a dorm room since she could have lived at home. She had just wanted to learn... be better than what she was.

Business wasn't booming and I had always managed to just eke by rather than actually get ahead. So Renee and I extolled Sammie Jo that if she wanted to go to college, she would have to pay for it herself.

She had taken up work over at the River Bend restaurant, an eatery that wasn't too far off the channel that led into the back lake. I had come in a few times while she was working. It had done me proud to see her working for what she wanted and that she was going to go much further in life than her old dad had gone.

Then came the day that she had taken her mother's car to work and I had never seen the car or her again… until yesterday.

Yesterday…

It already seemed like a lifetime had passed since my daughter's brief return and death. Maybe the reality was finally starting to hit me… Renee wasn't coming back and neither was Sammie Jo. I had my friends and neighbors sure, but it was up to me to raise this little boy and show him how to get by in the world.

Maybe I'd do a better job than I had with my daughter.

A storm blew in with the night; I had sat on the porch with Lincoln in my arms.

The boy was asleep while my old eyes had stayed rooted on the clouds, watching as the slow-moving thunderheads rolled in. There were flashes of lightning followed by distant tolls of thunder. I rocked back and forth and Lincoln kept sleeping content as dark night became momentarily illuminated with the flashes of electrical arcs, like God himself had a vendetta against the world.

"Maybe we'll see some ball lightning, huh?" I whispered to my grandson who continued to sleep. It was that quiet right before the sky falls out that was always my favorite part of a late spring thunderstorm... the tension, your hair standing on end, then you smell the freshness of the clouds...

Then it begins.

The rain came down in a sprinkling hiss that developed into a full-fledged roar, the lightning and thunder accompanying in a crescendo of heavenly fury.

I prayed there wouldn't be a twister. There had been one a few years back that had torn through the pine and cypress forests around Uncertain. I had seen the devastation up close; the trees torn up by their roots and thrown around like they were kid's toys. I wasn't eager to see that kind of power up close.

I hadn't bothered to turn on any of the lights in the house; the lightning illuminated the halls and rooms every time a thunderbolt slashed through the sky. I knew the pathways around my house by heart and walked with confidence. Sammie Jo's crib was sitting firmly in the living room and I laid Lincoln into it, the boy crawled and grasped for a moment before he lay still... calm.

The thunder boomed outside, and I sat back in my lazy chair, kicking the leg out and laying my tired body down to rest. I hadn't been able to sleep in the bedroom since Renee had passed. Too many nights I had rolled over searching for her only to find empty sheets.

Wonder what she would have said if she had known a grandson was on the way...

Those same thoughts accompanied me into the depths of sleep.

The howling wind woke me; I came out of good dreams of a happy family like a drowning man gasping at air and scanned the room around me.

My front door was open, the hinges squealing as it flapped back and forth against the wall from the gale outside.

Lincoln was still in his crib. I could see his little hands grasping at the air, gurgling noises of happiness.

I stood up, clicking on the lamp; the floor was wet. The rain washing through the front door had left quite a mess on the carpet, but that didn't scare me as much as the muddy footprints still wet and fresh.

There was nothing else that they could have been. An odd angular shape, round like whoever had made it had swirled their foot around on the floor to make their foot prints bigger, or they were trying to wipe away the evidence of their trespass.

There were several different paths, but the ones that ended at Lincoln's crib seized me with panic. my heart felt like it was in a vice as I stumbled to the gun cabinet and retrieved my rifle.

"*Who's in here?*" I roared the question as a challenge, but no answer was forthcoming from whoever had invaded my home.

I closed the front door slowly; the rainwater had made a mess of the footprints closest to the door, reducing them to nothing more than brown smears against the tile and carpet.

If the intruder was still in my house then the only way

CATFISH IN THE CRADLE

out was through the screen door that was directly in my sight. They could try to run but first they'd catch a bullet.

I checked the kitchen: nothing.

I crept through the hallways diligently searching each room: nothing.

There was no one in the house.

If my friends could see me, they would have brought the lab coats and the white vans. My paranoia was beginning to get out of hand; there wasn't anyone out there following me and my grandson, just an old man's regret.

The adrenaline left my system and I just felt tired.

The grief came, and I walked over to Lincoln's crib, letting the tears roll down my face. I didn't know when I would come to grips that my daughter wasn't coming back... who would raise my grandson if the grief killed me? I doubted I would live to see the boy get married, and if I did it would most probably be from a wheelchair, pissing in a bag with a pretty nurse wiping my ass.

That ain't living.

Lightning flashed, and something caught my eye outside in the dark.

There was someone standing on the hill leading down to the boat.

I immediately snatched up my rifle and threw open the screen door. The ancient glass rattled in the frame as the sounds of the storm hit me with the force of a cannon. The rain chattered against every tree trunk for miles, creating a staccato that I could barely hear myself over. The lightning flashed over and over while the thunder roared in fury.

The figure stood with its back to me. I could see the dirty jeans and jacket covering a hoodie pulled up to conceal the person's head. The shoulders were tall, broad; no way could it have been a woman. There was something odd about the way he was standing, slumped.

I shouted a warning over the gale, aiming the rifle at the man's back, but he didn't move.

I took a few steps closer and shouted again.

I was close enough to touch the man now and I shoved the barrel of the rifle into his back.

He toppled forward, the jacket sleeves fluttering in the wind.

It wasn't a man, but some sort of effigy or scarecrow propped up to simulate a man standing, sticks wound with strings of plant fiber to simulate a body, bits of leaves stuffed here and there... all of it painted with symbols I couldn't decipher.

The clothing was mine.

I recognized the tattered work jeans with the hole just above the knee and the frayed ends of the legs. The jacket was an old thing that Renee had given me and had been hanging in my closet, and the hoodie was the only one that I owned.

Someone had come into my house, someone had taken the clothes. I wasn't paranoid.

I retreated back into the house and waited for the storm to clear.

Didn't reckon I would be getting much sleep that night.

CHAPTER SIX

I CALLED OTIS OVER THE landline in the morning; he promised he'd come out as soon as he finished up some paperwork. Mist had risen up over the lake with the sun. The cypress moss was dripping, and the trees were long with shadows. The effigy lay where I had left it.

I was feeding Lincoln the formula that Sue Ray had left for me yesterday when I heard the tell-tale cough of the engine and saw Otis and Beau coming up the road. Mud immediately caked his brown boots as the Sheriff exited; Beau gave a long-suffering look towards the ground as his pristinely shined black shoes stained with the countryside perfume.

I carried Lincoln with me to meet both of them. We didn't bother shaking hands or making much small talk as I led them around the house to where the effigy was laying on the ground, damp clothes hugging it tight.

Otis carefully turned it over and chuckled. "Shoot, could probably win first prize at the fair this year."

I didn't bother telling him that I didn't think it was funny.

"Didn't see anyone set this thing up?"

I shook my head.

"And you were asleep when you say whoever broke in set this up."

Again, another nod. Otis frowned and asked to be let in the house to look at the footprints I had found.

"They're all rubbed around on your carpet. Can't even tell what kind of shoe he was wearing." Otis sighed and stood up, rubbing the bald spot on his head and looking supremely frustrated. "I'll grant you that something weird is going on here Grady, but there isn't much I can do besides get Beau to stay out here on watch and send that thing over to the Marshall PD."

The deputy looked sick at the thought of staying out here by himself for a bit, but I assured him that Gideon and Vicky had promised to watch Lincoln while I went hunting so he wouldn't be alone.

I didn't get my clothes back. "Evidence," Otis had told me as He, Beau, and I heaved the thing into the back seat of the police cruiser, readjusting it to fit thanks to its awkward shape. I was out of breath when it was over as it had required all three of us to lift and my heart was racing in my chest. Thought I would have a heart attack as I panted, leaning against the old scratched metal of the car.

Otis promised to check with the Marshall PD on the results of my requested paternity test. I hoped for a name, any bit of information about the man who had lured away my daughter.

They both left with Beau promising to come back later and take up his watch of my property.

Gideon and Vicky arrived a half hour or so later, neither of them caring how much mud splattered against the side of Gideon's truck. Vicky swept Lincoln up when they entered the house, cooing over the boy and bouncing him in her arms.

I clapped Gideon on the shoulder. "Look close, son. That's the future for you." Gideon's eyes were calm, like that was a joke he had heard plenty of times before. "Hopefully not for a long time."

I had seen Gideon Whyte grow up alongside Sammie Jo, one of the few people who grew up around here that stayed because they wanted to, not because they had to. He was a pretty successful fisherman and had landed spots on a few shows that had featured the lake. He was currently the record holder for the fourth largest fish ever caught in the lake. Honorable kid; never once forgot respect for anyone older than him.

I planned for a long day on the lake. A couple of cold Coronas (my favorite) went into the ice chest that had lost its deep blue sheen over the years from all the times it had played faithful to me under the hot bayou sun. Raw chicken in a plastic bag: gators couldn't get enough of it, flocking and tearing into the meat like it was open season. Turkey sandwiches, not bologna. I'd never like it that much. A couple of bottles of water.

After I was done, I went back to my bedroom and put on my waders. Renee had always immediately washed them when I had come in off the lake after a long day. She never could stand the smell of blood and fish guts. They weren't camouflage fatigues like the military; no these were more brown and khaki, easier to mix in with the woods around the river. I grabbed my orange hunting vest, sliding it easily over my shoulders..

Gator had been my primary source of food over the years, but like everyone who had grown up around here I had tried my hand at deer hunting.

I walked back out to the gun cabinet. Vicky had settled in easily on the couch with Lincoln in her arms. Gideon had made himself comfortable next to her and had turned on the TV.

Flashbacks to that same couch and Renee holding Sammie Jo in her arms while I fiddled with some carving or another. But I couldn't let the grief get to me if I wanted to eat this summer. I had to get going.

But I didn't feel like going alone.

"Vicky, I'm going to have to borrow your beau for the day if you don't mind. These old hands and eyes aren't what they used to be…"

People always felt sorry for the elderly. Maybe it was because my generation never really asked for help. Self-reliance had been our bread and butter.

Vicky glanced at Gideon, who shrugged. She smiled and sighed, "Oh what the hell. Y'all be careful though."

Gideon smiled and stood as I thanked his girlfriend and unlocked my gun cabinet, pulling out the two bolt-action .22s that I kept mainly for hunting game. The younger man handled it well. His folks had obviously taught him that a gun wasn't a toy but a tool; he checked the safety, made sure that it wasn't loaded, and angled it away from everyone in the room.

"Lock the door after we leave and don't open it up unless you know who it is. Beau will be by after a while to watch the place."

I saw a shadow pass beneath Vicky's eyes. "Expecting trouble?"

"Couldn't say just yet; just keep the doors locked unless you know who it is, okay?"

She said she would, following Gideon and I as we dragged the ice chest, guns, and the rest of the odds and ends out to the boathouse.

Gideon loaded it all into the 175 while I went to my workbench, grabbing rope, the giant pronged anchor that I used, a makeshift gator hook, and the necklace of gator teeth I kept in the little drawer beside the skinning table. It was half trophy and half good luck charm.

Gideon clambered into the boat as I activated the winches. The tightly wound metal wires groaned as they lowered the boat into the water. I walked onto the lower dock and stepped easily into the boat as Gideon pushed off the pier, propelling us back and into the channel that ran behind my cabin.

Vicky walked out onto the dock, Lincoln's hand clutched tight in her own. "There goes Grandpa. Say bye-bye!" She waved the boy's little hand at me, and for a moment I felt that flood of love you're supposed to have for children, especially your own blood.

The kid's face though, the closed eyes and pallid skin… the love soured into resentment just as quick.

They were standing on the exact spot where my daughter had taken her last breath.

I cranked the engine on and we sped away.

It took maybe a half hour to get to the big lake from my cabin. I cranked the motor into high gear and we rocketed down the channels and bayous, the lily pads, salvinia weed, and trees rushing by in a blur as the river narrowed and widened at random.

The big lake stretched all around us, rolling green hills with the barest glimpses of houses showing between their leaves taking up the view every which way you looked. Duck blinds dotted the waters of the lake, grey thatch and dried straw covering up the wooden piers so that any fowl lighting on the water wouldn't notice their death crouching behind the cover.

"Where'd you say we were hunting this gator?" Gideon shouted over the motor screaming behind us.

"Down at Long Point around Goose Island!" I replied, angling the 175 to the right, motoring close to the coast that would take us there.

CATFISH IN THE CRADLE

We were in remote territory now, and Gideon's cell phone barely caught reception as we disappeared into the cypress trees and moss. This wasn't a channel for tourist boats or party barges eager to enjoy the thrills of the lake; this was for hunters and fishermen eager to make their catch away from prying eyes.

Long Point had just started getting a few houses built, mostly rich folks who put in pools and tennis courts, little estates that they could disappear to from their high paying jobs in Shreveport. The marsh around Goose Island was a maze of cypress trees that hadn't been trimmed or cut to make a proper channel, every trunk haphazardly jutted from the water.

I throttled down and moved the boat deftly under moss, Gideon keeping a lookout for any cottonmouths that had decided to sunbathe on the branches.

A row of droplines were strung from some low hanging branches. I killed the engine, raised the motor, and let our wake push us forward. These weren't my lines, though I had a few strung up in various bayous. I mostly stuck to the river and various channels; the big lake had too much traffic.

Gators were opportunistic, and the game wardens would raise hell if the hooks got bigger than few millimeters across. A gator would swallow any fish and hook off a dropline without hesitation. I pulled up the line and was rewarded with the tattered heads of fish that had bit down and fallen victim to a reptile. Couldn't be sure that it was my gator, but considering the location and brazenness of attacking something men had put in the water… it was pretty damning.

A few fishermen I knew ran trotlines instead of drops. Matter of taste really, running horizontal hooks instead of vertical. More dangerous that way, though. An angry alligator would start thrashing as soon as they felt even the slightest bit of disturbance from the object keeping them there.

"Think he's still around?"

I glanced over at Gideon who was eyeing the .22 nervously. I shook my head at the boy, smiling ruefully. "Doubtful."

The boat rocked as I released the dropline back into the water. I clambered up onto the bow fishing seat and gestured for Gideon to take the twin seat on the bow.

I had installed a trolling motor to get through shallow waters; if we hit a stump with the main motor, we were going to be up the shit creek people kept talking about. I didn't feel like diving in this murky crap for a dropped off prop while a gator with a taste for blood was swimming around.

The motor vibrated, and we moved forward through the trees. It was slow going, barely more than couple of feet every thirty seconds. I was like a new man, out in my element and I felt ten years younger.

The rains last night had brought up the mist. It closed in tight around us like a lover. The shadows from the cypress, pines, and logs in the water loomed out at me. I took it slower than normal and more than anything I listened...

There was a distant and deep croak... bullfrog.

A splash or two as we neared driftwood in the water... turtles.

Then another noise, creaking.

Metal.

CATFISH IN THE CRADLE

I pulled the motor and swung the boat starboard. The mist parted, and the deep greens of the woods came into view… along with a small aluminum boat wedged haphazardly between two trees.

I cut the motor and glanced at Gideon who wordlessly reached down and grabbed the .22 rifle, working the breech and sliding a round into the chamber.

I didn't immediately reach for my own weapon; I looked around the shore for footprints or any sign of the boat's owner. Nothing.

"Anybody there?" My voice drifted through the trees, echoed across the branches, and disappeared.

Something obviously wasn't right, and my heart thumped in my chest, a sweat forming on my brow that had nothing to do with the humidity.

The remains of a net floated in the water along with a splintered paddle, tackle box half open, an aluminum fishing pole…

Someone had been here and got out quick.

I rustled around in the hull until I found my own paddle, gesturing for Gideon to keep an eye out as I reached out and attempted to dislodge the other boat from between the two trees.

There was a groaning sound, and the boat slid down, exposing the corpse underneath. The right arm was gone, bits of ragged blood and bone hanging like a wet rag from the stump. The face had been shredded, exposing jawbone with the lower teeth still outstretched in an unfinished scream.

"*Jesus!*" Gideon shouted, nearly tumbling from his seat while raising his rifle. I stared grimly at the torn orange life jacket; he had tried to swim for it.

Can't outswim an angry gator.

I raised my arm to my nose to block out the smell. The flies and mosquitoes had descended eager to make a meal of the unfortunate man, Minnows swam in out of the dirty red wounds while bigger fish darted in for swift bites, disappearing when I scattered them with a splash of my paddle. The buzzing was terrible.

"It fucking did this?" Gideon half shouted, his eyes roving over the dead man, fighting hard not to be scared. Good boy.

"Yeah, man-eater now."

"We going to report it?"

I shook my head; I had only ever killed one man-eater in my entire life on this lake. It had almost killed me then.

"State pays a higher bounty than old Miss Meyers, enough to buy Vicky a pretty little ring even if we split it."

Gideon didn't laugh. "I'm not planning on asking her right away, Mr. Pope."

"But you are planning on asking her."

I glanced at the dead man; the thing that had done it wasn't far.

"What about him?"

I bit my tongue. Guilt over leaving him gnawed at me, but I wasn't about to make myself a target or the kid with me.

"Leave him for now. We'll get set up, kill it, and bring him back with us." Gideon looked uncomfortable, and I didn't blame him. But dead was dead. He wasn't going to go through any more pain than he had already gone through.

There was a cypress tree not far away that would suit my purposes. The branches were strong and thick. They'd have to be for the thing I was intending on catching.

Gideon handed me the rope, thick half-inch yellow strands that I tied overhand and anchored to the boat. Then it was time for the bloody business. The icebox popped open, a trapped blast of cold air hitting my face, and I dug around a bit before I retrieved the Ziploc bag of chicken meat. When I had bought these cuts from Gabriel Nichols down the road, he had done his part to make sure that the blood and juices were still saturating the dead birds. Alligators love raw chicken, can't get enough of it, and Gabriel's chicken had always scored a high success rate with my hunts.

The hook pierced the meat easily enough. A little spurt of blood hit the water and floating like a smear on a canvas. I spun and tossed the hook up and over a strong branch, letting it slide down until it hovered right over the edge of the water.

"You be ready with that rifle Gideon. When it comes it's going to be quick."

Gideon nodded. He wasn't an amateur; he knew that it wasn't a game. I could count on him not to hesitate.

I washed my hands in the river. Nasty stuff to do in muddy water, but even if it was dirtier than a pig's ass, it was still a sight better than the feeling of blood running down my hands.

"If you're hungry, I packed some sandwiches, but watch yourself." Gideon nodded and immediately began digging through the ice chest, pulling out the sandwich and a bottle of water. I asked Gideon if he could toss me the same and he complied. Southern men can eat; never let anyone tell you different. The mist was still hanging over the water, but my watch said it was getting closer to lunchtime than breakfast.

A distant crow cawed while we chewed, but my ears never left that tell-tale dripping behind me. The blood seemed to be louder when it hit the water than any mundane morning dew.

The turkey was delicious and if Renee were alive would have skinned my hide for eating after washing my hands of raw chicken blood in a dirty river. I smiled as I took a drink of water; if salmonella killed me at this point then I could live with it. Lincoln would be better off in a home that actually had money.

The dripping stopped, and I heard a light splash. I looked over… and stared into the eye of the biggest gator I had ever seen.

Massive, ancient, awe inspiring… terrifying.

Its jaws clamped around the chicken like it was nothing. No more than few milliseconds must have passed, then it was falling back to the water, monstrous grin frozen in place.

I heard Gideon shout as the boat was rocked to the side, the gator trying to make a break underwater for the deeper estuaries. We were pulled like a toy. The boat anchor I had tossed out into the water keeping us in place, I braced myself in my seat as the alligator came to a jerking stop. Gideon gripped the sides of his chair, making sure the .22 he held was secure. I stood up and reached for my own rifle.

The water churned in front of us as the alligator discovered that its prize wasn't going to be as easy to eat as he thought.

There was a gunshot. Gideon was jumpy and already chambering another round.

"Wait until we haul him up! Might as well be shooting plate armor!" I shouted as I struggled to get my work gloves over my calloused hands.

The alligator's head appeared above the water as he struggled, massive teeth half the size of my fingers chewing through the rope.

Had to make this quick.

I gripped the rope and heaved with all of my might; it was like trying to haul blocks of cement. Except blocks of cement didn't have enough teeth to tear me limb from limb without hesitation..

The gator moved towards me, then it pulled away just as quick. This was going to be a fight to wear down the reptile's endurance, something I doubted that I had the strength to accomplish.

The rope frayed even more.

"Gideon, shoot it!"

The young man looked at me. "Thought you said to wait!"

I shook my head and hauled as hard as I could on the rope. "Forget what I said. Just kill it!"

He didn't hesitate and fired off a round. There was a small spurt of blood. Another round, more blood, and another… The alligator never stopped thrashing, hissing and roaring in anger as the stinging bullets punctured its hide.

I hauled as hard as I could and the gator's head stretched high. Gideon fired and its jaw spewed blood.

The rope snapped, the gator fell, and the water calmed.

I fell back panting, my heart pounding hard in my chest. Gideon was pale, his rifle scanning the water back and forth, on guard for any further attack from the massive reptile.

"That thing was a twenty-footer." Gideon panted.

I shook my head. "Don't let your imagination get the best of you, son. It was fifteen feet at most."

Gideon looked at me like I had lost my mind. "That's still bigger than any gator I've ever seen on this lake!"

I nodded my head, sighing as the last bubble disappeared from the top of the water. "Yeah me too."

CHAPTER SEVEN

WE TOOK THE DEAD MAN with us. I tried to bundle him up in a tarp that I used to cover up the boat when I went hunting on the lake islands. Gideon had been a bit squeamish, and I wasn't at all comfortable. I had closed his eyes, but I could still feel that accusing stare beneath the lids.

Gideon and I didn't talk on the way home. I think he was still a little in shock about his first dead body. After the Robichaudes, my stomach didn't exactly turn at the sight of the dead, through a meat grinder of teeth and scale or otherwise.

We pulled into the bayou leading back to Carter's Lake without incident, rounding the turns and channels through the cypress trees until my home was in sight.

Vicky must have heard the boat motor because she was opening the backdoor and walking out with Lincoln grasped tight. Beau emerged from the side of the house. The grim looks on our faces and the fact that I didn't head for the boathouse but instead for the shore darkened the young woman's features. As soon as I cut the motor she immediately asked. "What happened?"

Gideon hopped out of the boat and embraced Vicky, uncaring of how he smelled or what had happened. He was quiet, but I could see the barest speck of tears spiraling down his cheek.

Nothing wrong with that. Cry away, Gideon... I had the first time too.

Beau stepped up next to me and I shrugged my shoulders at the tarp in the bed of the boat. "Help me with this, Deputy?"

He silently stepped up next to me and cast a curious eye at the tarp and then back to me. Yeah, he wasn't going to open it here, not with Miss Vicky Barnes standing in full view and unprepared to see a mangled corpse.

The Deputy picked up one end and I picked up the other, carrying it back to Beau's truck. Beau lowered the tailgate and I gently slid the tarp in.

"What's this all about Mr. Pope?"

I grasped the corner of the tarp and pulled up, exposing the victim for him to see. I watched Beau stumble back in revulsion, his hands immediately finding his knees as he dry heaved and waved his hat trying to cool down.

"Gator attack. Found his boat too... tiny thing, barely half the size of the monster that killed him."

Beau panted and nodded his head and I let him catch his breath. Poor boy lived in a town where nothing ever happened like this... at least it hadn't for a long time.

"You realize that Otis is going to put the word out on

this… every gator hunter in the state is going to be on this lake inside a week."

Oh I knew, but that just meant that I was going to have to find the fucking thing and kill it first.

Scott Carter came back out to retrieve the body; Otis came with him after he heard just what it was that I had fished up.

Neither of them said anything when they got out of Scott's truck or when we shook hands. I could tell that Otis wasn't thrilled to be picking up another body on my property.

One is misfortune, two is suspicious.

Otis went to talk to Beau while Scott joined me at the back of the Deputy's truck. The wounds would bear out that an alligator had killed him. I didn't know the man, which meant he was either a tourist or lived in one of the other small townships bordering the lake, and I had Gideon to back me up. Either way I would be in the clear.

Scott had come prepared with a body bag, and when he saw the extent of the injuries his eyes darkened. "Damn…"

I nodded somberly as he zipped up the bag.

"How big did you say the gator that did this was?"

I told him of my estimate and Scott shook his head in amazement. "Hard to believe that dinosaurs are still roaming the Earth. Am I right?"

I nodded in agreement, my mind immediately trying to formulate a plan to kill the beast before the yokels descended to steal my payday.

"I'll take him in to Marshall, see if we can get an I.D. He didn't have anything on him like a wallet, did he?"

To my knowledge he didn't, but I hadn't gone checking the man's pockets either.

Otis sauntered up and unzipped the body bag just enough to get a look at the unfortunate man's face. "Poor bastard." A sentiment I agreed with.

Otis asked me where I had picked the man up, and I regaled him of the day's adventure.

"Well Grady, I'm going to have to—"

"Post a bounty and get the game wardens on it, yeah I know… just gives me impetus to work harder."

The Sheriff grinned broadly. "Hell Grady, you've got about a day's head start. You know Larry and Desmond ain't going to do shit about it for at least another day."

Larry Knowles and Desmond Miles, our local game wardens, were usually more concerned with busting folks for having too many people on their boats versus hunting down man-eaters. Good guys and sharp too, especially when we gathered for Saturday poker night before church in the morning. But it was the assholes who'd speed up and down the channels eager to kill for a little extra cash lining their pockets that worried me.

"Beau is going to stay out here for the rest of the day, make sure that no one comes traipsing around your place."

I thanked Otis for the consideration, unsure that anyone was going to try anything while the deputy bumbled around my property, easily spotted.

CATFISH IN THE CRADLE

"While I'm out here, might as well tell you that we need to start thinking about funeral arrangements for…" Scott paused and licked his lips, clearly uncomfortable.

My grief had turned to stone in my belly. She had come back and left just as quick, leaving me with the consequences of her choices. A parent's role I guess, cleaning up the mistakes of our spawn.

"I'll stop in next time I come to town, probably tomorrow if that'll work for you," I said.

Scott agreed that it would, getting into his van to take the dead man into Marshall. Otis didn't move, and I could see that he still had things to talk about.

"What is it?"

The sounds of Scott's truck engine was beginning to fade, and Otis took off his hat to wipe the sweat on his forehead. "Listen Grady, this isn't going to be easy to hear but I got the test results back for your paternity test… inconclusive on the father's part. Whoever he is, he's not a felon."

It wasn't as soul crushing as I thought it would be. Maybe it was because I had a giant reptile to focus my rage on, a true blue-collar Moby Dick story… one of the few movies I actually enjoyed. Gregory Peck's performance was flawless.

Or maybe it was because I had a grandson to take care of and God had saw fit to keep me in the dark about his father lest I become a murderer.

"Grady, you okay? Anyone home?" I came back to myself and realized that Otis had put a hand on my shoulder, probably his idea of sympathy.

"Yeah I'm fine. Just thinking."

Otis cracked a smile. "Well don't strain too hard. Fella like you might hurt yourself!"

When I didn't smile in return Otis nearly deflated. "Listen Grady, I'm not too good with grief and all that, makes me feel uncomfortable, but I'm your friend. You know that, right?"

I did know. I just wasn't in the mood for jokes.

"You call me if you find anything else or you get in trouble out there."

A few more pleasantries, some goodbyes, and Otis left.

I wanted to sink down into my chair, but Gideon and Vicky were still inside. Gideon looked shell, shocked his eyes wide and staring at nothing.

Vicky walked around the room toting Lincoln and when she heard the door closed and saw me walk in, she nuzzled my grandson affectionately. "There's Grandpa. Look, there he is!"

Had Renee cooed this much over Sammie Jo when she was born? I couldn't recall, but then again there were a lot of things that I couldn't recall… side effects of the passing years.

"Thanks for watching him today, Vicky."

"No problem Grady. The little guy and I have bonded!" She nuzzled my grandson affectionately again, eliciting a happy gurgle from the little tyke and a weary smile from me.

"Were you like this the first time?" His voice was harsh; hollow… like words were foreign things that he had just learned how to use. Gideon looked up at me. "Was it this bad for you the first time?"

The image of the Robichaudes swinging from the rafters, faces distorted and bloated came to me, and I nodded my head. "Yeah. Yeah, I was."

"Does it get better?"

Wasn't so good at sympathy, never had much of it myself, but I patted the younger man on the shoulder and tried my softest voice. "Yeah it does."

Vicky laid Lincoln back down in his crib and went over everything she had done to take care of him that day. "A few home ed classes really helped in preparation for this."

I didn't want to hug her, didn't want to make her uncomfortable. After all, she brought me my usual breakfast and I might have needed her to babysit again.

Vicky accepted my thanks and hoisted Gideon up off the couch. He was still lost in his own head, but his color had returned along with a small measure of strength.

"Vicky, when you get home you take care of him good. Haven't seen a man with his courage in a long time."

It was one of the highest compliments I could give, and I meant it. Gideon had been cool under pressure, and I wished I could take him back out for a second crack at the monster gator. I knew better than to push him. I had seen men and women break from things less than what he had seen today, and I had seen just as many find their bravery and come back ready to wrestle the fear back into that deep corner where it had come from.

Gideon was one of those men who would come back.

Once again, I thanked Vicky and they left. I saw them to the door and shut it behind them, not bothering to see if they made it to Gideon's truck or not.

I washed my hands in the kitchen. If I needed to pick up Lincoln I didn't want to infect him with anything. The restless bug was in me and even though my chair and a round of FOX News sounded good, I couldn't relax.

The nagging thoughts on how to catch the gator ate away at my mind.

Good time for a walk then.

When Renee and I had stress or problems in our marriage, I had gone for a walk. Major decisions featured a walk. Financial struggles: walk. It cleared the head, lessened the stress that came with the tides of life, probably because I had other things to focus on while I took in the great outdoors.

And this time my newborn grandson was coming with me.

I changed into clothes that weren't stained with chicken blood: jeans and an old work shirt that I didn't mind getting dirty. An old hat to cover my eyes from the sun and a car seat that I could carry Lincoln around in and I was ready to go.

My grandson was passive in his crib, snatching at the blankets and moving his small feet around as he explored the world around him. His eyes were open and his cheeks pudgier. I don't know what they were putting in the formula these days, but I could swear that he had lost that wrinkled newborn look despite being days old. I picked him up gently and placed him in the car seat, strapping him in so that he didn't roll around and harm himself.

I opened the back door and walked out onto the hillside. The boy wasn't heavy. I had carried far heavier through thicker terrain once upon a time… Now it was time to decide on which direction to go.

Walking around to the front of the house I noticed loyal Deputy Beau Caldwell leaning back in the cab of his pickup, eyes closed and blissfully snoring. My tax dollars at work, and my already low respect from the man continued to head south.

Cy's cabin caught my eye, the brown wood and dirty windows poking through the trees, beckoning for me to come and take a look. I hadn't been up that way in a long time. Painful memories of my dead friend and the long humid nights we had spent drinking on his porch shooting the shit usually made me avoid the place like a plague. Pretty sure that it had fallen into disrepair, which kept anyone from buying it. Young folks were looking for homes that didn't require any work, a situation that suited me just fine since I preferred my privacy.

The pine trees that mixed with the Spanish moss had left a fine coating of dead needles across the forest floor. Bright green poison ivy brushed against my pant legs as I made my way through the underbrush, the unused path that I had once kept neat and tidy overgrown through the years of disuse.

An irritated squirrel raced up a tree near me as I brushed the moss out of my way and walked up the small hill to the cabin. Cy had never been one for yard work and dirt more than grass held sway now.

"See this Lincoln? An old friend used to live here." It felt strange talking to the boy. My own voice was like an alien thing to me; I never spoke to myself when I was alone, and even though Lincoln counted I still felt like an idiot squawking to myself.

The boy made gurgling noises and ignored me.

I stepped up onto the porch, a modest-sized area that had been cleared of all the furniture that had once been so familiar. Used to be a grill over by the railing overlooking his long walkway that led out to the river.

Probably sold off to some yuppie now. Cy had never married or had kids… Renee and I had been the closest thing to family, but he had neglected to leave a will. Probably hadn't seemed important to him until the end.

The man had smoked cigars, and I could still see the tell-tale burn marks in the woodwork from his repeated extinguishing of the burning luxuries.

Tobacco stains and good memories… I missed the man.

Peering through the glass was like staring through time that was missing a few things. Cy's furniture had disappeared, vanished into the ether of his estate sale, but the appliances, the wallpaper, the little things that had made this place home was still intact. Covered by a fine layer of dust but still intact.

More memories of better times, I sighed and stepped away, picking up Lincoln's carrier and walking back towards the front of the house. I ran my hands along the ancient wood, savoring the coarse feeling on my skin.

The SOLD sign in the front yard stopped me in my tracks.

Couldn't be…

Who would have bought this place?

The young thing with the pixie cut and fake smile on the sign told me nothing. Whoever bought this place was in for a hell of a shock when they realized how much their new neighbor wished they weren't there.

I spit at the base of the sign and turned away to walk into the woods.

CHAPTER EIGHT

WATCHING FOR SNAKES IS A must when you go into the woods: copperheads hiding amongst the leaves, cottonmouths in the trees or streams, and timber rattlers waiting behind logs. Every step I took I watched for them and spoke to my grandson about the dangers of the woods and river… all the threats he was going to become intimately familiar with as he grew up.

I walked close to the river, maybe a half-mile or so away from my house, enjoying the sounds and smells that came with this place, distant birds, the sweet smell of flowering trees, and the heavy scent of the river.

Despite the seeming peace, I felt uneasy that feeling of being watched like a hot lamp on my face. There were no footsteps, no figures in the trees, no distant sound of dripping water.

But I was being watched.

Not a lot of folks came out this way. The salvinia covering the water and turning the place into a gigantic bog full of dangerous depths and turns. The channels had to be routinely remade as nature crept back in, the only constant the ancient logs with the markers.

One in particular though gave me chills, as it did for everyone else who saw it. Channel marker 158 wasn't much different than the other markers the state government had erected across the lake, made from oak like the rest, bolted with signs to show the boat roads like the rest…

No other channel marker had quite the body count though.

It was accepted fact that marker 158 had once been an ancient oak that stood on the edge of Jefferson, Texas, a scant stone's throw away from the lake.

With a twisted sense of justice, it had been used to execute all manner of folks… criminals, degenerates, and the occasional black who got a little too handsy with a white woman for his own good. It wasn't the law's justice, it was the people's justice. And since when does the mob know who's really to blame?

Then mysteriously, the gallows tree was cut down in the 1997 by parties unknown. Too much shame and blood mixed in its branches for the well-to-do civilized people in town, disappeared and forgotten about.

I remembered reading about the event, how the state government vowed to find the culprits who had desecrated their precious historical site, how nobody had ever been charged.

CATFISH IN THE CRADLE

By all accounts that should have been the end of it.

Until it had mysteriously appeared along with dozens of others. The marker system officially ended at 150, but the placard hanging off the ancient wood told a different story.

It had been the focus of diner talk and speculation for these past twenty-one years. I'd heard everything from government cover up to alien intervention. Nobody knew for sure.

I stared at that channel marker now, wondering if and when it would ever rot away. If it did, it would certainly ease my conscious.

Under the numerous amounts of graffiti and vandalism, odd symbols and carvings had been etched in the ancient wood, symbols that hurt the eye and shaped in ways that didn't have precise angles or meaning.

I had tried pronouncing a few once since I thought they were words threaded through the carvings, and I found that the odd cadences and rhythms hurt the back of my throat and came out as gibberish akin to a croaking gurgle.

This place made me uneasy, so it was no wonder I felt like I was being watched. It bothered me that I had drifted here in my aimless walking.

Even worse, Lincoln had suddenly become active and was straining with his tiny arms towards the channel marker, sitting ugly in the middle of the river.

"No, no Lincoln, you don't want any of that. Trust me."

His mother had been fascinated with this place too. I had forbidden her from coming up here, but she had disobeyed so much I had just given up on it. She had brought her friends to drink and play all, under the watchful eye of marker 158.

I glanced down at my grandson and wondered if history was going to spit in my eye once again. Shaking my head and still feeling uneasy, I turned for home.

There was a light splashing, like a fish biting at the surface of the water.

I jumped and whirled around my mind conjuring up all kinds of terrible images about what was behind me. I saw a shape in the water, a deep shadow that banged against the channel marker. I tensed, my teeth gritted as I waited for it to breach the surface… had to be an alligator; that was the only thing massive enough to create such shadows.

It turned slowly and bobbed to the surface.

I looked at waterlogged bark instead of scales.

Just a log, probably tossed into the water by lumberjacks up river.

I let out a long harrowing sigh, and Lincoln giggled in his carrier. Little bastard.

Hefting the carrier, I turned for home and screamed, throwing myself to the ground as something massive came flying through the air, crashing through smaller trees and branches before landing with a resounding *thump* against the ground.

I lay panting on the ground. Lincoln was bawling his eyes out, and I reached out and dragged the carrier close, looking all around me.

The water-soaked log was lying a few feet away, still rocking from its flight.

I scrambled to my feet and looked back at the river.

CATFISH IN THE CRADLE

The formerly still waters rippled out, trying to calm themselves again.

There was a sound, a deep throated croaking...

I picked up my grandson and ran for home.

I didn't stop until Cy's cabin came back into view. I nearly collapsed when I finally came to a stop.

I was winded, gasping for breath as I dropped Lincoln (harder than I meant to) onto the ground and fell to one knee gasping for air. If my coach from high school could have seen me, old and desperately trying to heave air down my throat, he would have died of shame. As it was his corpse was turning in his grave over at the Marshall Cemetery.

My grandson was bawling his eyes out and I tried my best to comfort him, but all I could manage were a few cooing wheezes that did nothing to stifle him.

I was afraid, not ashamed to admit it.

The locals down at the bar talked. Everyone usually had a story about some strange thing they or their second cousin had once seen. Devil Monkeys, monster fish, honest-to-God aliens, and motherfucking Bigfoot... gentleman and lady alike all had a tale to spin over drinks. You couldn't live on this lake and not have a story or two, and I had often been a listener, laughing at the punchlines and calling bullshit at the exaggerations.

Never thought I would be the one with the strange story.

Couldn't rationalize it and couldn't think of anything strong enough to throw a log a few dozen yards from the river into the woods. But I still wasn't ready to believe in Bigfoot. I hadn't reached that level of crazy yet.

I got my breathing back under control—hard thing to do when you are pushing sixty)—grasping at Lincoln's carrier and rocking it back and forth. "It's okay, you're okay, we just had a little scare is all."

"Hey… mister you okay?" There was a man waving from the back of Cy's porch, young with a parcel of unruly brown hair drooping just below his ears.

I waved a hand to let him know that I was alright, The wind still knocked out of me.

He vaulted the railing, landing in the grass, and rushing over and crouching next to me, a firm hand placed on my back. "Just breathe in deep Mr. Pope. You look like you had quite a scare."

I looked up into the young man's face. A scruffy beard that looked like he spent the majority of his time trying to tame, piercing green eyes, dirty pants and shirt.

His accent though, Cajun… couldn't be.

"You… aren't…" I managed to gasp out; the young man smiled and gently helped me to my feet.

"You haven't seen me since I was small; found me at the old homestead after…"

He didn't need to say anything else. It was him. He was back. Last I heard he had been raised by kinfolk down in Lafayette traumatized but alive.

"I owe you my life, sir."

CATFISH IN THE CRADLE

Luc Robichaude, second youngest son and only survivor of his family, had come home.

CHAPTER NINE

LUC PRATTLED AROUND IN MY kitchen, mixing together things he found along with ingredients that he had brought in his car. I had caught my breath mostly, my heart slowing into a steady beat, though I still had some tightness in my chest.

"Keep going at that rate Mr. Pope and you're not going to make it to sixty."

The younger man shoved something hot into my hands that I tried to grip; the cup trembled in hand… my nerves were still on edge.

"Drink it up and you'll feel better."

I sniffed at it, a bitter scent filling my head. "What is it?"

Luc winked as he settled into the chair across from me. "Momma's own cure all, guaranteed to settle hangovers and soothe the soul."

Mumbo jumbo juice; now *that* I understood. I sipped at it—some kind of hot tea by the taste—and the more I drank the more I calmed down.

Luc watched me with a careful eye. "See something out on the lake Mr. Pope?"

"Monster gator on the loose Luc. Fifteen-footer... man-eater." I managed to explain the encounter Gideon and I had while I greedily finished off the last of the tea. There was no more tightness in my chest.

"Was that why you were running?"

"Yeah," I lied.

"Going to have to be careful then when I go down to the dock."

The clues I hadn't exactly pieced together fell into place. I was a little slow on the uptake, but it made sense. "You bought Cy's place?"

Luc nodded. "Couldn't move back into the old place, you know?"

The burned cabin and the dangling bodies flashed behind my eyes "Yeah, I know."

"Sammie Jo around? Or Miss Renee? I never did ask you if this little man is yours."

He must have seen the look on my face as he ripped open fresh wounds without even realizing it. "I'm sorry Mr. Pope."

I gritted my teeth and tried to hide the tears, staring at Lincoln, my dead daughter's birth screams replaying in my head.

"Renee passed last year sorry to say," I managed to get out moving on to my most recent pain. "Sammie Jo was kidnapped, or ran off, couldn't say which yet... then she came back..." I couldn't go through the whole story, not again. I just gestured to Lincoln. "This is her son."

Luc didn't draw attention to the tears or my feeble attempts to hide them; polite boy. His focus was entirely on Lincoln.

He wiggled a finger above the newborn's face. "Hello there, little guy. Your mom and I were friends… went way back…"

He was a year younger than Sammie Jo. Though I couldn't tell, I thought I could see the vague hint of tears on his face, but it might have been a trick of the light.

Lincoln's head lurched all of a sudden, mouth snapping around Luc's outstretch finger, an innocent growling cooing from his lips as Luc snatched his hand away. My grandson giggled, and I smiled at his spirit. It was only then that I noticed that Luc looked troubled, a small frown adorning his face.

"What's wrong?"

The Cajun man looked at me and the frown disappeared, happiness returning. "Oh nothing I'm just not used to kids."

That was a fair reason. I wasn't exactly used to the boy myself.

Luc stood up, wiping his finger clean of Lincoln's drool. "Well I think I'm going to get back to moving in my things, making that place livable… holler if you need anything Mr. Pope."

I grunted and set the tea aside, struggling to rise out of my chair and shake the man's hand. "Luc, you're old enough now that I think Grady will just do fine."

He shook my hand, firm grip. "Grady, then." The younger man smiled, promised to check in later, and left.

I sighed and sat back down in my chair. I'd have to feed Lincoln later. That way he wouldn't scream to high heaven and keep me from enjoying what little peace I had.

The thoughts of the alligator consumed me. I couldn't leave Lincoln alone to go hunt. If anyone stopped by, child protective services would be all over my ass... or, knowing my luck, the house would burn down from a freak brush fire.

Couldn't push Gideon too hard to go with me. He needed time to recover. If I had to hunt it myself I would, but the old muscles weren't what they used to be, and the reptile's newfound bloodlust would make it ten times more aggressive.

It wasn't going to stop either. When an alligator got that size there, were only four things it could eat to satisfy its hunger: deer, cows, other gators, and people.

Which one do you think is the easiest to grab?

It would kill again, and soon.

I'd get Luc to watch Lincoln tomorrow, hunt it on my own. After the word went out today there would be plenty of other folks out to make a quick buck.

Whatever my new neighbor had put in my tea soothed me. The warm spring air crept into the room around me and I felt at ease... I couldn't think about what had happened at marker 158, the event becoming the furthest thing from my mind.

Instead I thought about my new neighbor, grown into a man from the scared little boy I had found with bruises knees and tear tracks down his ash-covered face staring at the charred carcass of his home.

The sound of creaking wood woke me. Warm air and my chair had a way of luring me to sleep faster than anything else. It was sometime in the late afternoon. The light had shifted across the walls and made interesting patterns of shadows across the wood.

My annoyance grew as I wearily tried to shut my eyes again, figuring that the wind was blowing and my old home was just breathing to let me know she was still standing.

It didn't go away, though. The creaking continued.

I grunted in annoyance, Lincoln must have been up and ready to be fed. It was a little surprising that the boy wasn't crying, but what did I know? Sammie Jo had been quiet many times when she had been hungry.

I opened my eyes and looked towards the crib and yelped in surprise, practically falling out of my chair.

Lincoln was standing in his crib, hands grasping the rails, eyes wide with excitement. When he saw I was up, a mouth full of teeth cocking into a wide grin.

This wasn't a newborn; this kid could have been two or three years old.

"G'mpa, G'mpa." The kid blubbered the words and pounded at the edge of the crib with his two meaty hands.

I found my voice. "Lincoln?"

The little boy laughed and jumped up and down in the crib. His skin was more pallid, so pale to be nearly grey with a dark head of hair unlike his mother, eyes that were so dark I didn't think he had an iris until I saw the dark green around those black pupils.

He was naked, the little diaper and onesie Vicky had put on him in tatters by his feet.

"What the fuck?"

The little boy giggled at every word I said, relishing my voice.

He reached out his hand towards me. "G'mpa!"

I felt like I needed to vomit as the world swirled around me. This couldn't happen…

But that feeling that had itched at the back of my mind had been right. My grandson was a fucking freak and had killed my daughter. This only confirmed it. Screw mercury poisoning and whatever other tripe Scott could peddle. This *thing* had killed her.

"G'mpa!"

"*Shut the hell up!*"

The little boy looked shocked for a minute, his eyes widening, mouth trembling in fear as he started to bawl.

"No, no, you don't get to cry!" I shook the edge of the crib. "*Shut up! Shut up!*"

The kid just screamed louder and shirked away, huddling at the edge of the crib.

I wondered what I would have done in that moment if a rhythmic knocking hadn't diverted my attention.

CATFISH IN THE CRADLE

The pounding at the door startled me, and I glanced at the kid squalling in the crib. I wrestled down the fear, anger, and disgust I felt before grabbing my .357 revolver from the gun cabinet.

I said no trespassing and I meant it. If it wasn't someone that I was familiar with then they were going to have thirty seconds to vacate my property before I began shooting. I couldn't maintain civility or politeness when the little freak that was my grandson had aged two years in a matter of hours.

Another round of polite knocking happened before I reached the door. I unlatched the deadbolt and twisted the locks, opening the door just a crack.

A man stood on my porch clad in a brown suit that looked like it had gone out of style in the seventies. When he saw the door open he lifted the matching fedora off his head and clutched it to his chest.

"Pardon me—" He paused, his mouth opening and closing. "Sir, if I could just take a moment or two of your time?"

"No you can't. This isn't a good time—" I moved to shut the door and his foot darted out lightning quick and blocked the way.

"I'm sorry, sir, but I'm afraid that you haven't heard the details of what I'm selling."

His face was a pallid and unhealthy looking grey, like Lincoln's but more pronounced. His neck looked like he was suffering from gout; his chin melded straight into his neck that seemed to inflate as he took deep gasping breaths.

I placed the pistol directly into his smug face; he broadened his smile without showing his teeth. His mouth looked stretched like putty rather than natural, and it sent chills down my spine.

"No reason for hostility, sir. I'm merely here to inform you that I represent your grandson..." He stopped talking and his eyes bulged, looking every which way before he blinked. "*Lincoln*... that's the name... yes... I represent his biological father's family."

My eyes twitched, wanting to look back at the living room and my grandson, who had stopped crying. But if the years had taught me anything, it was to never turn your back to anyone who put you at unease.

"What did you say your name was?"

"I do apologize, Grady Pope. I did not properly introduce—" Another pause. "Myself. My name is Savant Huber." He flipped his crumpled fedora towards me, his stringy slick black hair doing little to disguise his rampant hair loss.

I recognized the name. "Any kin to Ray Huber down in Mooringsport?"

Savant smiled. "Yes, yes, sir. My great uncle; his brother's daughter was my mother."

Didn't care about family history too much. The Hubers were well know brewers of bathtub gin out in the bayous, selling on the fly to riverboats down in Shreveport.

"You a lawyer or something?"

Savant bobbed his head, the motion short like a dog watching a ball instead of a real agreement. "Or something indeed, sir. Lincoln's father's family sent me... you might have noticed some oddities...?"

I lowered the gun but kept it close. "Maybe."

"Ah yes. Well it is part and parcel of—" His damn pauses were beginning to unnerve me worse than his appearance. "His family. Quirk in the seed, I'm afraid. And he *will*—" The man emphasized the word in an odd, unnatural cadence. "—need to be remanded into their custody so he can learn how to live with his—"

My blood was running cold as his eyes twitched every which way before that putty smile stretched again. "—defects, yes." Whatever smile he was trying to project was about as convincing as an alligator grin. It looked somewhat human, but still projected false assurance.

I was surprised that the anger, the fear of my grandson, all the emotions that had boiled inside me minutes earlier was gone. You didn't admit things were wrong with your kin, and you didn't give them up.

You lived with it. You didn't acknowledge it. You dealt with it.

Blood isn't always thicker than water around here, but it was a damn sight thicker than this stranger on my doorstep. Couldn't discount it as just one more little oddity from the womb, one I could figure out on my own without this strange man.

"I appreciate the offer, mister, but I'm going to have to pass. Lincoln is just fine right here."

The man's foot didn't budge. "Now Mr. Pope, surely you've seen how fast he—"

"I've seen it. I've also seen a seal man and a bearded lady. He's a little different…that doesn't mean he needs to be with his deadbeat dad."

Savant Huber shook his head. "No, sir, you don't—"

I leveled the revolver back in his face. "You have thirty seconds to get off my property."

All manner of civility, and hell, *humanity*, disappeared from the man as his arms shot out and gripped the sides of the doorframe. A warbling croak bellowed out of his throat. *"Give him to me, Grady Pope!"*

I shot over his shoulder and he flinched away, retreating to the edge of the porch, his crumpled fedora falling from his hands. He shivered, his wide eyes blinking in the sun. "Give him to me, Grady Pope…"

"G'mpa?"

I glanced behind me; Lincoln was standing in the hallway, eyes wide.

Pounding footsteps and Savant Huber was rushing the doorway, a warbling hiss escaping his lips.

My aim was off, and I shot him in the arm. The revolver clapped thunder and the man fell back on to the porch screaming—it sounded like a yowling cat—and grasping his arm. I slammed the door closed locking it.

I swept Lincoln up into my arms as I passed and carried him into the kitchen where I could get a view of the front porch. It didn't provide a full view, and from this angle all I could see of the man were parts of his leg and feet. He stood up and I could see the end of his arm dangling, blood running down his arm.

It didn't look right. There was something in that bright red blood, streaks of grey that shimmered under the sunlight. Couldn't tell what it was, but damn, nicked an artery maybe.

CATFISH IN THE CRADLE

Where the hell was that deputy?

The man disappeared from my view. A few seconds later and he was running past the kitchen window, leading down towards the bayou. I could still hear him: "*Give him to me, Grady Pope, give him…*"

I covered Lincoln's ears and ran to the window, seeing the edge of the brown suit disappear behind the house.

I was scared, and I wasn't afraid to admit it. Men had tried to kill me before, but none had run laps around my house while trying to steal a child.

He kept repeating those calls, demanding I hand over my grandson. I expected to hear the tinkling sound of breaking glass, but it never came. Savant Huber's calls grew fainter and fainter, and then disappeared completely.

I breathed deep and Lincoln rested against me, trembling just as much as I was.

"G'mpa?" I quieted the boy, whispering that it would be all right.

More knocking on the door, and I tensed up before I heard Luc. "Grady? I heard a gunshot. You okay?"

"Yeah!" I called, my voice a little gruffer than I preferred. "There's a fucking lunatic running around outside!"

I heard Luc stumble on the porch, looking around. As I ran back to my bedroom and sat Lincoln on the bed, I pointed a finger right under his nose. "Don't move, you hear me?"

The boy trembled and didn't answer. he now looked two years old. I wasn't sure what I was expecting, but he'd grown a few feet and started walking in a few hours. Hell, maybe he could speak.

I left him there and hurried to the door, unlocking it and making sure Luc was alone before I joined him outside.

The hot day was the same, the long shadows and humidity unchanged, but now with an air of oppressive evil. I looked for Savant Huber behind every tree and errant moss strand. I briefly explained what had happened to Luc and he began looking around, fists clenched.

Deputy Beau Caldwell was not at the corner of my property sitting in his truck. In fact he was nowhere to be seen, gone back into town or to lick his own asshole. My already dismal opinion of the man plummeted further, and I resolved to tell Otis that if the little prick came back around I was going to kick his ass.

I told Luc to keep watch while I went back inside, momentarily glancing down the hallway at my closed bedroom door, overgrown grandson beyond it.

Couldn't afford to think about that right now as I unlatched my gun cabinet and pulled out a small .22 Sig Sauer. I handed it to Luc when I went back outside. He hefted it, checked the chamber, and clicked the safety off, pointing the gun at the ground.

Good kid.

There was something on the ground. That odd-colored blood. The dust had lapped at it thirstily, but there was still a distinctive trail that led around the side of the house.

I gestured silently, and Luc nodded, following in my wake as we rounded the house. There was a splattering against the wood right under the kitchen window, trailing back down and into the grass. We followed it around to the backyard; it led back down to the lake.

I scanned for a boat or anything that indicated where the man had come from. I hadn't heard a car engine or boat motor, and only a crazy person would dare swim through this bayou. Wouldn't put that beyond what Savant Huber was willing to do based on the few minutes of bat shit crazy I had experienced.

Something rustled in my boathouse. I glanced down the hill and there was the barest hint of movement in the gloom.

Luc followed me as I walked down the hill, blood droplets clinging to the grass like morbid little stars.

I stopped short of the boathouse door; I usually left it open, a bad habit that had led to snakebites a time or two and a lot of dead serpents. It was an old instinct to watch for danger, and right now it was screaming at me that Savant Huber was standing on the other side of the wall in the dark, ready to bash my skull in as soon as the back of my greying hair was visible.

"I'll circle around to the corner, cover you," Luc said.

I nodded and took a step forward, trying to keep my gun steady despite my nerves.

The dark doorway drew closer, inches away. I probed the inside of the doorway with the bottom of my foot and with a deep breath plunged into the thick of it, trying to flick the light switch on as fast as I could. The dim bulb sparked to life with a hint of ozone and I aimed the gun around me wildly.

There was no grinning maniac with a hammer, no brown-suited lunatic holding his bloody limb.

I was hit immediately with the smell. If anyone has ever cleaned or touched a fish, they were familiar with that stench. It was strong and pungent; biting into my nose like someone had been squatting in my boathouse and cleaning fish all day.

I heard dripping water and looked over at the edge of my boat, right behind the engine where the dock met the water.

Luc came in behind me, but I didn't bother turning to look at him. There was the brown suit and fedora by my boat, damp with blood and water, but Savant Huber was nowhere to be seen.

"Bastard is running around naked in the woods."

Luc didn't laugh, and I wasn't sure why I myself had stated the obvious. The situation was so strange I was falling back on something familiar rather than rooting myself in the now. I was scared and I'm not ashamed to admit it.

Then there was that nagging feeling in the back of my head.

That Luc Robichaude shouldn't know about Lincoln.

Couldn't blame my instincts; lynch mobs had been formed for less, and that protective instinct beat strong in my chest... mixed feelings about him aside, he was still the son of my daughter and my blood ran in his veins.

For the first time I thought that I would die for that kid.

Couldn't rightly explain it.

"This is... concerning."

I glanced at Luc, who had furrowed his brow. "You're telling me. You aren't the one who had a nutcase trying to break in and steal your grandson."

Luc abruptly stood, and I heard him muttering under his breath. It was too quick a snippet really, but the words were clear.

"This isn't like them."

Isn't like who?

"Luc?"

My friend and new neighbor shook his head and tried to give me a reassuring smile. "Who is the sheriff now? Might want to get him out here on this."

I voiced my disagreement. Otis was a friend, but he wasn't exactly decisive when it came to shit like this, and he'd already been out here more times than was kosher.

Once is misfortune, twice was suspicious, and three was grounds for arrest. Couldn't afford to be locked up in the old folks' home… not now.

Luc sighed heavily and raised his hands in surrender. "If your head's set then I'd say keep a steady watch in case he comes back. But what man would come back after getting shot?"

A damn crazy one.

I also wasn't born yesterday.

"What do you think this is, Luc?"

I watched his reaction to the question. Years of poker playing with Cy had given me a keen eye for spotting tells, and Luc's eye twitched before he responded.

"I think a crazy guy wandered out of the woods and took a shine to your house."

Good excuse, but he was still hiding something.

Luc smirked, and an evil look passed over his face. "I do have an idea though that will discourage anyone coming around here looking for trouble."

I was harsher than I meant to be. "Like what?"

"I'll let Mojo out for the night."

"Mojo?"

Luc nodded and helped me to my feet. "My mutt, big bastard, could rip through a grown man if I told him too… call up to the house if you need to go wandering tonight. He isn't too keen on people he doesn't know."

That nagging paranoia ate at me and I wanted to thank Luc for his help, but it didn't feel like help.

It felt like he was trying to keep me from leaving.

CHAPTER TEN

LUC HANDED ME MY PISTOL back and headed for home, telling me to call if anything else out of the ordinary sprung up. I thanked him for his concern and shut the door, leaving me once again in the silence of my home.

I immediately ran back to my bedroom looking for Lincoln. He wasn't sitting on the bed and I thought the worst: Savant Huber had managed to break in and kidnap him, he had lured me outside in collusion with Luc to steal my grandson for God knows what.

My heart was pumping out of my chest. Everyone was going to know now that my daughter had given birth to a freak… they'd take him away, stick him in a lab and inject him with all that shit that government people love to play with.

Running water and the sound of giggling.

The master bathroom connected into the bedroom. In my marriage, I had been confined to a tiny sink in the corner with one drawer that had contained my beard balm and other things that Renee had insisted I use, despite my admonition that they weren't anything but yuppie nonsense.

I walked in and the churning of bathtub water hitting porcelain assaulted my ears. The water was steaming but Lincoln didn't seem to mind he splashed and laughed in the bathtub without a care in the world. He must have heard me enter because he began excitedly laughing and pointing when I came in. "G'mpa, G'mpa!"

I crouched down next to him and smiled, swirling the water with my hand. "Yeah, kid. I'm your grandpa."

Night came quick; I had found some old clothes that I thought Lincoln could fit in. Occasionally Renee's brother brought his kids over to have a "real outdoors experience". That had resulted in a lot of discarded hand-me-downs over the years.

He may have been big enough to crawl out of the crib now, but I didn't have a bed that could safely hold him… so it was just going to have to do. I laid a pillow inside along with a small blanket; Lincoln was immediately on his feet when I sat back in my chair a few feet away. "G'mpa?"

I reassured him that I wasn't going anywhere.

Shit… I didn't have any kids' toys. The thought fluttered into my mind like the soft brush of bird wings and I smiled. Why was I thinking about children's toys when my grandson had miraculously grown in a few hours?

From somewhere distant I heard a rumbling bark; a long and distant howl followed then silence.

"Probably Mojo, boy." My grandson had looked at the window, startled.

It was a full moon tonight; a wind had come in from the north and was howling with every gust. The shadows of the trees contrasted with the shining bright water. A beautiful sight, for sure. Used to sit out and watch the stars under nights like this. A man could find peace by looking at the heavens in times of woe.

That habit had died over time.

"Mama?"

I looked at my grandson, my fingers tightening around the chair arms "What?"

Lincoln grasped at the air, his brow curled in confusion, his eyes looking around. "Mama?

I wondered how the kid even knew how to talk. It was damn peculiar, like he came equipped with the entire damn English language… though he had grown a few years in a few hours. So knowing how to talk was barely registering on the scale of strange shit.

"Where Mama?"

I gritted my teeth and shook my head, "Mama's not here."

The boy still looked confused and he spoke in a lighter tone, questioning. "Where Mama?"

I heaved myself out of my chair and wrapped Lincoln in my arms, bouncing him up and down. "Mama's not coming back."

He began to cry a weak, whimpering sound, and I felt the hot tears fall against the nape of my neck. I let the boy cry. I didn't think that he understood, but I couldn't be sure. Either way I let him cry, and I let my own tears come unheeded.

We walked around the house and I began to whisper to him all the things that this house had seen, about his grandma and how she would have loved to see another child come into the house, about his momma's victories and defeats.

The boy stopped crying. I could feel that light breathing that comes with sleep on my shoulder, and I walked him back into the living room, sighing deep.

I wasn't cut out for this kind of thing, I just wanted to sleep through the night. I had assumed my child rearing days were done, but yet here I was laying a two-year-old magically grown in just as many days back into a crib that he had already outgrown.

How was I going to explain this to my neighbors? It wasn't like I could just trot him into church tomorrow. "Hey Rev, this is my grandkid and I need him dedicated, growing boy and all. Did I mention he was born Thursday?" They'd burn him at the stake and stone me for raising such an abomination.

Or at the very least think I was crazy.

I sighed, and it was enough for Lincoln to wake up from his short nap. He looked around and smiled. I smiled too as he frantically pointed at the river.

"Yeah I'll take you out there, you're going to be one hell of a fisherman."

CATFISH IN THE CRADLE

"*Papa!*"

I froze, and my hands tightened around Lincoln's small body. "What?"

My grandson giggled again and grasped desperately at the sliding screen door. "*Papa!*"

I dropped him into the crib as gently as I could and whirled around, not knowing what I expected to see at that glass door.

The clouds were obscuring the moon and casting the night in eerie half-light and shadows, but I could still see the outline of someone at the top of the hill. He was tall, tall enough to scrape the ceiling with the top of his head. I couldn't make out a face or anything descriptive, but even that outline looked wrong, the head oddly shaped, dangling limbs that ended in something wide and club like, thick legs like miniature tree trunks.

He raised a massive hand that widened enough to create a small umbrella of darkness. There was a low throaty vibration, and I felt afraid. I crouched close to Lincoln, shielding him from seeing the man.

"*Papa, Papa!*"

There was deep groan, like ancient boat timbers rocking, and then suddenly a louder bark. That booming bark came again, and the misshapen silhouette of the man's head turned to look up the hill.

The stranger wheeled away, and I rushed to the glass window. The man moved lightning quick, his form doing an odd hopping gait before vanishing into the shadows and water.

I then saw a gigantic white form prowl by the window and a deep growling. Mojo on patrol. Thank God. The dog disappeared down the hill in pursuit.

I rubbed Lincoln's head and whispered an old hymn until he was asleep. Envied the boy; there was no way that I was going to be catching any sleep that night.

CHAPTER ELEVEN

PEOPLE NOTICE WHEN YOU DON'T show up to places that you had frequented near every day since you were thirteen. Folks get worried, and when folks get worried, they come to check on you.

I should have expected that, should have prepared. but when that nine in the morning knocking on my front door rattled in my ears, I knew that I had screwed up.

Lincoln lay asleep in the crib and I had spent the night watching the moon rise over the trees. The knocking made me jump and stare before I heard the self-confident voice of Davis Trucker. "Grady, the missus was worried. Thought I'd come by."

Sometimes that neighborly spirit bit you in the ass.

I stumbled over to the door and braced myself against it my tired bones doing little to keep me on my feet.

"Yeah..." I coughed, my voice a little hoarse. "Feeling kind of under the weather... thanks for coming by."

"Ah shit..." I could practically see the big man's face turning down in an expression of sympathy. "Need some help? I mean I know you have the kid with you and—"

I cut him off. "No, thank you. I'm good. Just going to make some of that herbal tea Renee liked and rest for the day."

"You're not feeling too good, are you?" He replied, his deep voice rumbling.

"No not really..." I was practically sweating. I had never known Davis to be a paranoid man, but I thought from the tone of his voice that he could sense I was hiding something from him. He knew where the emergency key, was and if he wanted he could have opened up the door despite my protests, just to make sure I was safe and sane of course.

After what felt like an eternity, there was heavy sigh on the other side of the door. "Well holler if you need me. Also, Scott was in the restaurant this morning. Told me to remind you that he needs you to come by the funeral home when you get a chance."

I told him that I would and that I appreciated him stopping by. The panic inside me began to subside and I breathed a sigh of relief when I heard the old Buick engine backfire and trundle away.

I nearly slumped against the door in relief and turned around to find Lincoln staring at me in the hallway. "Stranger?"

His words were getting better.

"Yeah it was a stranger, buddy."

The boy laughed and smiled those big black eyes staring in wonder. "Friend?"

"Yeah, kid, he is…"

The car seat that I had brought him home in was now useless. I didn't really want to go into town, but what choice did I have? If I didn't go to town, then the town would come to me and see things that I preferred to keep hidden. Taking Lincoln into town wouldn't remove suspicion, but it could diminish it. I couldn't readily explain a two-year-old at my home, but I could pass him off as a relative.

I took a deep breath before I opened the door. Lincoln walked passively beside me, his eyes scanning the trees like they were alien things that he was experiencing for the first time.

"What that, G'mpa?"

I looked down, and in the bright light of day realized that my grandson looked more unnatural than I had initially thought when I had brought him home. It was almost like looking at a character from an old black and white movie. His skin was so pale, eyes and hair as black as the night.

The boy grimaced at the sun. I walked him as quickly as I could to my truck and strapped him into the front seat.

I quickly climbed into the driver's seat. "Ready to go?"

My grandson wasn't looking at me. He was looking at the distant muddy river behind the house, his eyes a glistening sheen as his mouth flopped open, bits of drool slopping out of his mouth and onto his shirt.

I suppressed the shudder that ran up my spine and keyed the ignition, heading towards Uncertain.

I hadn't realized the weight that had been hanging over my mind until we left the cabin behind us. I felt relieved, like the river that I had spent my life on was an infected vein that I had cleansed from my system.

Should have listened to that instinct and run far away. Should have taken Lincoln to the middle of the damn desert far away from the strange shit that had seemed to infest my life since my grandson had come into it.

Scott ran an old school funeral home, with living quarters over his mortuary where he worked. We had played cards a few times over at his place. I had never felt quite at ease whenever I went there. Always creeped me out that there were dead people in the basement.

We weren't far away from the old Longhorn Ammunition Plant, an old factory that the U.S. Army had operated until the nineties, when they had discovered that different toxins were leaking into the groundwater.

Good riddance; the place had always been an eyesore and had practically poisoned the lake before they had started cleaning it up. Now it stood like an open wound, sinking into the swamp slowly but surely, scavengers combing the old ruins for every scrap of value that was left.

I glanced at the old place through the trees. Lincoln seemed fascinated, his small hands and face pressed up against the glass and mewling and grasping as the faded grey concrete vanished from view.

I turned into Scott's driveway, black asphalt leading up to the two-story house that backed up against the cypress trees and steep embankment leading back down to the river. Scott kept his lawn well-manicured, the grass a shimmering green, and Misty had procured all kinds of decorations in shades of red and blue that made the place seem much more hospitable than it actually was. A sign proclaiming CARTER FUNERAL HOME sat on an island that the drive circled around. I circled the drive until the tailgate was pointed towards the house and killed the engine.

"Lincoln listen to me." The boy was enraptured with the trees and didn't look at me until I repeated myself more forcefully and grabbed his chin, which was covered in slobber. "Lincoln, I need you to stay here. Do not leave the car, okay?"

The boy nodded. "Okay, G'mpa."

I was damn sure that the kid was just repeating what I said so I had brought a distraction. The stuffed animals had been his mother's, a pink horse and a grey elephant... I handed both to the boy. "Play with these until I get back."

Lincoln laughed and eagerly grabbed the toys out of my hands, making gibberish noises that I couldn't decipher. I shrugged and suppressed a grin. I stepped out, locking the door behind me, my grandson oblivious in the cab. Didn't intend on being here long for the grim task of deciding how I wanted to bury my baby girl.

Dead ivy as brown as fall leaves clung to the white edifice, making it look like the windows of the house were crying muddy tears. I walked up the cracked brick steps and knocked on the front door.

There was a blurring motion behind the black window and a click as Scott opened the door. "Morning, Grady."

I was taken aback. Scott usually looked cleaner cut than this. He had heavy bags under his eyes, and his normally well-maintained goatee was beginning to show the hint of a five o'clock shadow as whiskers crept across his cheeks. I had expected him to be wearing his Sunday best, ready to head on into church and receive a touch of the Holy Ghost. Instead he was dressed in a long-sleeved, dark grey shirt and black sweatpants.

He must have seen my questioning look as he attempted to force a grin, but there was something more, something he wasn't telling me. "The missus isn't feeling well so I think we are going to skip out on the service today."

"Brother Arnold will be upset." I grumbled. The younger pastor had been a point of contention amongst some of the older parishioners, who grumbled that a city boy like him didn't know how thinks really worked out in the sticks.

"He'll just have to admonish us next Sunday. Besides, Misty's vomiting up her guts this morning. I had the worst dreams, if you couldn't tell."

Oh, I could tell, but it would have been rude to comment. Instead I simply asked him if we could get down to business so I could get my own tail to church. I had no intention of examining the Good Book today, but it made a convenient lie to get my friend moving. I'd ask for forgiveness in my nightly prayers. The Lord was just going to have to understand.

CATFISH IN THE CRADLE

My friend looked like he wanted to be anywhere else but standing in front of me. That nagging sensation that had been chewing at the back of my neck since he had come to the door practically screaming at me.

"Scott, what's really wrong?"

He sighed and gave me the most apologetic look that I had ever seen in a man. "Just brace yourself, Grady."

I didn't ask what he meant as he let me in and we walked down the dimly lit hallway towards his basement door. His home was old with drab wood furnishings and carpet that had once been the height of refined, but now looked like it had come from era before Civil Rights. Scott and Missy had decorated the halls with old family photos that displayed scenes from distant childhoods long gone.

I had already been a young adult by the time these pictures were taken, but I remembered the time very well. A time before everyone walked around with a phone chirping in their pocket, a time when the world hadn't seemed so vile and decrepit. Often thought that the older you got the more you realized how much of the muck and shit you had to crawl through to get anything worthwhile and then by chance or reason it broke your fucking heart.

Scott led me down into the basement, and every step was heavier as I descended, like little gremlins were running around adding weights to my feet. My heart pounding in my chest as my friend reached the bottom and clicked on a small bulb that bounced on the end of the cord.

Muddy water covered the floor and a massive hole in the wall a little taller than me split the linoleum to the left. I could see the faint shimmering of water and dangling roots; a tiny cave beneath the trees behind Scott's home. Could have happened to anyone, but Scott's face told me that this wasn't the end of it.

"Think the storm weakened the wall from the extra water, but it didn't cave in until last night."

The damage didn't look too bad. A thin layer of algae covered the floor and some of his equipment, but nothing that didn't look fixable.

Scott's ashen look made me realize that it was much more serious, and the realization hit me like a bag of hammers.

"Where is she?" I managed to croak out, my voice hoarse like my vocal chords had been scraped bloody.

My friend had tears in his eyes as he blinked twice. "The water was over my head when I found it and when it drained out…" He could barely continue, his teeth gritted like he expected me to hit him. "She's somewhere in the river now…"

I blinked, and I felt the hot tears spill unheeded from my eyes. I turned, saying something about needing air and stumbled up the stairs, my feet pounded on the floor, echoing a staccato beat like a demon's laughing.

I burst out into the humid air and vomited all over Scott's porch. It came bitter from my throat, and vaguely I was aware of Scott's footsteps and his repeated, "I'm sorry!" I couldn't tell if he was crying or not. All I knew was that my baby girl was now a nest for minnows and fish… that is if the gators hadn't gotten her.

Scott was quiet, and I straightened myself tall. Never let them see you bleed had been a mantra for a long time, and my friend had just seen me at one of my most vulnerable moments. He wouldn't dare pity me it had just been a moment of weakness.

I turned slowly, and Scott glanced at the pile of vomit. "I'll clean that up, Grady. I understand that you're upset and I'm sorry… I didn't know this would happen."

Maybe it was a blessing that what came next happened, or else my mouth would have said some things that I would regret down the line.

Whatever anger I had was lost by the sound of my truck, open door alarm pinging. I turned slowly, revelation anointing me before I saw the open truck door and the discarded grey elephant and pink horse.

"Lincoln…" I breathed out before I tore down the brick stairs, sprinting to my truck.

"Grady, what is it?"

I ignored Scott as I scanned the ground, looking for any sign of where my grandson had disappeared to.

There was nothing.

I prayed, closing my eyes and mumbling platitudes to the Lord, hoping for an answer.

"Is it Lincoln? Was he in here?"

I continued to ignore my friend and pray… then came the sound of splashing. It was faint, but I could hear it: rhythmic and repeating, and I thought I heard a small voice speaking in stilted little words.

I sprinted towards the sloping riverbank, grasping at the trees for balance as I hit the edge of the slope.

"*Lincoln!*" I screamed at the top of my lungs and was rewarded by a splash of water so loud that I was sure the kid had fallen out of a tree he had climbed into the water.

Then I heard the muffled sobbing and splatter of water. I took a deep breath and climbed down the embankment. Lincoln was at the bottom, obscured by old driftwood, tree roots, and water grass. His back was to me; clothes caked in the grey mud and clay.

"Lincoln?"

The boy splashed the water with his hands like he had lost something, frantically grabbing at the mud. An ancient and dry reed snapped under my foot and the boy whirled around.

I recoiled.

His eyes were dilated so extremely that the white wasn't visible, just the massive black pupil and the olive green iris around it.

Gigantic night crawlers wriggled in his mouth.

The worms twisted and turned, and Lincoln smiled at me as he chewed. Thick black guts oozed out of the worms and ran down the boy's chin in filthy brown rivulets.

I rushed forward and grabbed the boy's chin in my hand. "Spit it out!" The boy snapped at me, his teeth chomping down on my finger, drawing blood as he greedily gulped down the worms and made sucking noises that sounded vaguely like croaking.

A bullet would do right about now, pressed against the little monstrosity's eyes, a trigger pull and more blood in the muddy bayou.

CATFISH IN THE CRADLE

The boy finished gulping down the last wriggling night crawler and stared into my eyes with those gigantic black orbs. A weight passed between us like an itch on the inside of my head.

My anger and fear melted away, and as the boy reached up to me I took him into my arms. "Let's get you out of here."

"Grady?"

I froze in my tracks; blood running cold in my veins as I slowly turned and saw Scott standing at the top of the hill.

"Is that Lincoln?"

I could lie, but what would be the point?

"Yeah, yeah it is."

Scott seemed in awe as I climbed back up the embankment with the boy in my arms. "Wow, he's gotten big since the last time I saw him."

This wasn't the reaction I was expecting.

"Listen Scott you can't tell anyone. Folks around here aren't going to be so understanding."

Scott looked confused. "What are you talking about?"

I gestured with my shoulders at my grandson. "He's grown two years in two days; how can you not notice!"

Scott's look of confusion darkened his eyes dilated and his voice came out in a dead drone. "Grady… you've been raising Lincoln for two years. He didn't just magically grow up overnight."

I was stunned, amazed at the ridiculous bullshit that I was hearing… I was old not senile. "Don't feed me that horseshit Scott, I was here to fucking arrange for my daughter's burial!"

Scott kept that same smile, bland and alien on his face as he repeated the same thing. Lincoln giggled in my arms; the boy was looking intensely at Scott, almost enraptured by the man. Scott kept repeating that Lincoln hadn't aged overnight, that it was all in my head.

He followed me to the truck repeating it.

The words were echoing as I put Lincoln in the car and drove away, Scott disappearing in the rearview mirror… I could still make out the words.

CHAPTER TWELVE

I WAS CHILLED TO MY core, and maybe my denial about everything that had happened in the whirlwind of strange shit that was the past two days had finally reached the point of no return. My daughter's body taken by the river, a log thrown at me by nothing, Savant Huber, Scott acting like he had been fucking brainwashed…

The boy eating worms.

I drove home in silence, occasionally glancing at the boy still caked with mud, sullying the cab with its baked and rancid smell.

How was I okay with this? I had denied and pushed away problems with his mother for years, and that had led to disaster. I was aware that this wasn't natural, my suspension of disbelief strained to the breaking point.

Hadn't been intending to go to church this Sunday morning but when it came to matters beyond this world, I couldn't think of anywhere else to seek answers. The Good Shepherd comforted me, in times of woe and turmoil the Lord had always seen me through.

I'm not going to lie and say I was the most devout or even the best Christian. Usually I left God at the church doors on Sunday, drawback of being brought up in the church rather than finding it on your own. Lack of zeal.

The First Baptist Church of Uncertain was an old, single-sanctuary white building with a decaying steeple and faded paint that really needed a touch up. But the collection plates had been a little light this month as folks desperately clung to their meager paychecks. There wasn't a parking lot, just a grass field that backed up against a vast pinewood. People in this part of East Texas often called it the Pine Curtain; the forest seemed to stretch on forever and concealed all manner of activity, both legal and criminal, if you knew where to look.

"G'mpa?"

I ignored the boy as I found a parking spot at the edge of the fleet of cars that were spread in neat lines across the grass. It was a good turnout today for a congregation that usually boasted a few dozen at most.

Killing the engine, I lifted Lincoln from his seat and carried him towards the double doors, eager to see my return to that old time religion.

The service was in full swing. I could hear the piano and choir singing praises while the congregation's voice droned along in blissful monotone. My heart thumped as I took each step up to the double doors, unsure of what I expected to happen. Maybe the congregation would rip us both to shreds, but more likely they would ride us out of town... a freak and his sire.

The doors opened and Lincoln squirmed in my arms, wriggling like a fish to get away and run back to the truck, his grunting cries drowned out by the sound of rapture.

Earl Ray and Sue were on the third row back. Our game warden Larry Knowles and his wife Kathy sang from the hymnal, their nine-year-old son Eric looking bored out of his mind.

I hung around at the back of the sanctuary, gazing over the parishioners as the music ended and Pastor Arnold Kizer stepped up to the pulpit. With his young and confident voice, he asked for those who were in need to come to the altar.

There was a weight on my mind, like a riptide in the ocean urging me to come... to lay my worries down. Every inch of the back my head blazed with pain, every step forward comfort...

As I walked down the aisle with the dirty kid held in my arms the singing slowly stopped. This must have been a shock for my friends and neighbors who knew me to be a back-row Joe, unlikely to ever be bold enough to reply to an altar call. There were hushed whispers and murmurs amongst the crowd as the gossip machine went to work. I didn't care anymore.

I knelt at the altar, the boy's black eyes staring all over the place, those deep throating grunts in his chest. I prayed to God, Renee, Sammie Jo... anyone who would give me peace and wisdom to process what had just happened.

Lincoln's cries reached a crescendo and died away just as suddenly. I felt a comforting hand on my shoulder.

I opened my eyes and Pastor Arnold was there. "Blessed be you, Grady Pope, that you have brought a child to be dedicated to the Lord this day."

Arnold's dark brown skin mixed with the grey clay covering Lincoln, and he smudged the sign of the cross into his forehead, the boy's head turned every which way before he closed his eyes, seemingly at peace.

"May I, Brother Pope?"

I nodded my head and he lifted Lincoln from my arms. A sense of relief had come over me like I had delivered my grandson from eternal damnation and into the arms of the loving God.

That same weight and itching feeling came back twice as strong, and then another feeling like cool water running through my mind, two forces fighting for supremacy and resulting only in a splitting migraine. Clutching my head in pain I looked up at Arnold Kizer on the pulpit, clad in his best Sunday suit, all chocolate skin, kind honey eyes, and well-maintained black beard.

I blinked and his skin was flaking in horrible rashes, honey-flavored eyes transformed into beady black orbs, dark writhing gills on the side of his neck, his mouth filled with pointed needle-like teeth, spilling a torrent of water onto his frayed blood stained suit… squamous skin wriggled beneath the ancient fabric.

And what he held in his hands…

CATFISH IN THE CRADLE

It stretched a long slime and mud-covered hand, a webbed and repulsive thing that stroked the monster holding him. There was a hissing sound, and a dark rippling purple tongue writhed like a night crawler dug up from the earth.

I blinked again, and only Pastor Richard was standing at the pulpit, smiling serenely, Lincoln grasped tight. My migraine was gone; the only thing left that heavy feeling in my head like I was congested.

"From the precious water I baptize you... may the Lord in his mercy keep you and set straight your path."

From somewhere a bowl of water had been produced, and the Pastor was washing my grandson in the waters, the grey clay flaking off and exposing his pale skin.

I was surprised that the boy wasn't fighting. I had never seen a two-year-old so calm.

Arnold's confident voice reached a crescendo. *"It will come about that every living creature which swarms in every place where the river goes will live. And there will be very many fish, for these waters go there and the others become fresh; so everything will live where the river goes."* He brought Lincoln out of the water, clean, his pale skin and clothes drenched. "Praise our Father!"

Most of the congregation clapped in slow robotic motions, their faces slack and bored minds already focused on where they wanted to eat but a few... a few cheered like they had just seen the second coming of Christ.

Arnold gestured to me and I rose from the altar. He handed Lincoln back to me, words of blessing that I didn't really listen to.

"Go in grace my friends!"

The service was over, and there were myriad murmurs and idle chatter as people began to funnel out of the sanctuary. I had come for answers about my grandson and had instead dedicated him to be baptized.

What the hell was I thinking? The plan had just been to sit at the back of the sanctuary until the service was over... not prance down the aisle like it was Main Street and they were serving pancakes at the end.

Lincoln hugged me tight and I realized that he had fallen asleep despite everything. People crowded close, eager to see the boy held in my arms.

"Oh he's a cutie pie!" Miss Franklin who ran the Uncertain Fishing Co. exclaimed as she gathered close.

"Just like his mother." Nate Biers, a fisherman who had grown up with Sammie Jo.

More people crowded around, parroting compliments like they were going out of style.

The reverend stepped in, hands outstretched as he ushered them back "Do not... crowd the man, he's had a long... day."

His speech had an odd cadence that I hadn't noticed thanks to my head feeling like it was about to split down the middle. Needed to drink more water instead of the sauce.

The parishioners wished me well and left while Brother Arnold threw an arm around my shoulder. "Don't mind them... Grady Pope... let's go... back to my... office."

I couldn't feel his touch through my jacket, but it still sent shivers down my spine. My temporary hallucination was already a fading memory, but the recollection of those webbed inhuman hands holding my grandson was enough to make me choke down bile.

It had just been a hallucination. Stress caused that, right? All the shrinks I had ever seen spoke of trauma and painful circumstance messing with your head.

Never thought it would happen to me. Renee in her last days had urged me to see a therapist to deal with Sammie Jo's disappearance, but I had always thrown the idea away. I was too prideful to admit the problems that plagued my family, didn't want some jumped up shit with a doctorate rustling around through my head. Besides why pay a man to tell you that if you had been better your daughter wouldn't have run off and gotten herself killed?

Renee had wanted to go, to get help for the sadness building in her, but I had held her back. If anyone had gotten word it would have been the talk of the town: the Popes were messed up in the head. Allegation and assumption was currency around here rather than fact.

Probably why Renee had gone from a beautiful matron to a corpse in months. All the sadness had built up and killed her. Leaving me with the grief and bitterness.

There was a small parsonage attached to the church. Brother Arnold and his wife Jeanette lived a modest existence; The parsonage was just a small living room, bedroom, kitchen, and study combination. Many a prayer group had been led from that living room. Renee and I had attended a few when the feeling that we needed to be better church people hit us before inevitably letting our attendance fall by the wayside as life intervened.

Jeanette appeared from the kitchen. With honey skin and dark curls swirling, she wore a burgundy dress and matching heels. She smiled brightly when she saw Lincoln held in my arms.

"Oh my goodness Grady what a… wonderful child. Haven't seen him since you brought him by to see us two years ago."

I was beginning to feel like I was on the butt end of some joke. The kid had been born two days ago and was speaking. Nobody around here including me were brain surgeons, but observation should have tipped anyone off that this wasn't normal. And I most certainly hadn't been by to see them before this moment.

"Jeanette… could you… take the child?"

I took an involuntary step back and Arnold held up his hands in placation. "You and I are going to take a walk Grad. Don't worry. Jeanette has helped rear a few over the years."

The pressure in my head returned, overriding my instinct that was screaming for me to run and not look back. I realized that Arnold was right. What was I expecting? The pastor's wife was going to run off with my grandson? Ridiculous.

Jeanette reached out and cradled Lincoln. "We have a bed for him. I'll put him there while you boys talk."

Arnold smiled and patted her shoulder. "Thank you, sweetie."

She winked at him and walked away, cooing to my grandson as the pastor gestured for me to follow him. We walked down a long hallway to a side door that he opened, waiting politely for me to exit the parsonage.

The backfield leading to the pinewoods stretched from the door. I breathed in that fresh smell, attempting to stifle my headache as Richard politely shut the door behind us.

"I know you have questions Mr. Pope."

"No shit, Preacher." Renee had always made me watch my language, but after everything, to have someone acknowledge that something was off was gratifying, relieving. I wasn't crazy.

I was so wrapped up in my own thoughts and the damn migraine running like a freight train through my head that I missed what the pastor said and apologized.

"It's this damn headache. I uh… well, I'm sorry to say I've been hitting the bottle a little harder these past few days."

My cheeks flushed red; odd feeling to be embarrassed, but you just didn't go around admitting to preachers that you were taking extra rounds of the devil's piss to forget your troubles.

"There's something to be said for water and life, Grady. Come on."

He headed towards the forest and I walked beside him, a shepherd and his wayward goat. I stood a good few inches taller than Arnold, the top of his head barely hitting the bottom of my mouth if we were to stand toe to toe. Despite that, he walked like a man who had all the answers.

Where he was taking me was at the edge of the woods, just beyond the tree line. I had always been jealous of the folks around here who didn't have to buy their water from the market. Drawing it out of the ground saved on the paychecks.

The well was a square block of granite, overshadowed with a wooden roof to prevent contamination. It had an old pulley system for drawing up the water adorning the wooden plank crossing between the two beams. I could see the old ammunition plant distantly through the trees, the off-white walls peeking through the green and infecting the atmosphere of the place.

"The church has been out here a long time. Was taking one of my prayer walks when I found it. Drink up. It's good, clean stuff."

I drank deep from the bucket; the water ran clear and was much cleaner than anything that flowed through the river. Arnold continued to talk as I drank. I didn't really pay much attention; my headache was blazing in my head.

Arnold spoke of all the times over the past few years that he had seen Lincoln, funny stories full of so much horseshit that I could practically smell it. My memory had been going these past few years, causing me to doubt myself often enough, but I knew beyond a shadow of a doubt that I hadn't been raising this boy for two years.

But the fact of the matter was, everyone else seemed to believe I did. If I didn't play along, then I was more than likely to be spending the rest of my days eating through a tube and paging a pretty nurse when I needed to piss.

At least for now.

I smiled at the preacher who returned it. "Always used to think you people gave out 'feel good' advice that didn't actually mean anything. Thought I was going crazy there for a minute."

I let the bucket drop out of my hand and the weight propelled it back down into the well. There was distant splash of water and it put me on edge. Couldn't be sure whether the man bought it or not, but I didn't plan on staying long to find out.

Jeanette was rocking Lincoln in her arms when we returned to the living room. My grandson looked peaceful in her grasp and Arnold clasped my shoulders. "So a man-eater on the loose? Figured you would be all over that."

Jeanette looked up her eyes a mask of wonder. "Yes it was the talk of the congregation this morning, a man dead… it is quite the sensational bit of news isn't it?"

Their comments sent chills racing down my arms as I tried to maintain a serious look, each of them talked like they were fucking robots with occasional moments of sense.

Arnold joined his wife in cooing over Lincoln. "Half the boys in service today were eager for me to wrap up and get out on the lake. Bounty is three thousand dollars, payable by the state."

He looked up at me. "Why don't you join them, Grady Pope?"

I looked at Lincoln and shook my head. "I really can't, Lincoln—"

"Well we can watch him, can't we, Arnold?"

"That we can, Jeanette!"

There was no fucking way I was leaving my grandson in these people's hands. "Well I mightily appreciate the offer, but Victoria Barnes already offered to watch him today."

Arnold smiled. "But of course. Do come back if you need more time, Grady. We worry and care about all members of our flock."

I told them I would and picked up my grandson, getting the hell out of there.

Still felt their eyes on the back of my neck as I left.

CHAPTER THIRTEEN

IT WAS VICKY'S DAY OFF from serving the patrons of Shady Glade. Davis always shut down on Sunday out of respect for the Sabbath. Folks were always disappointed, but there was both River Bend and Bayou Landing if you were in desperate need of some food.

She had a small house up the road in Uncertain, directly next to the old motel that had tried to be something fancy once upon a time. Nice place, modest, hell of a lot better than where I lived. Vicky had planted flowers that bloomed violet, relishing the spring rain that had rolled through. I pressed the doorbell and stood back away.

Vicky was clad only in a t-shirt that reached down just above her knees, old football shirt by the look of it, with the number 43 emblazoned across her breasts. Gideon appeared behind her, clad only in a pair of dark navy boxers.

Didn't think that most people were aware that Vicky and Gideon were shacking up. If they did, their reputations would be shot around town, any respect faked with a veneer of politeness.

Gave her a comforting smile. Wasn't in my nature to narc on some young people living their lives. Couldn't judge either; Renee and me's indiscretions had taken place on the bottom of a boat deep in the bayous, moans of pleasure mixing with the bullfrogs.

"Sorry to interrupt you on your day off, Vicky, but I really need someone to watch him."

Saw the younger man visibly sigh and temporarily felt the guilt wash over me. He'd seen things that no one should have had to deal with and was getting comfort the best way I knew how. Then came the old man with the kid who needed help. Swore I'd make it up to him.

Then came the magic words I had been hoping for. "What the hell happened to him?"

Vicky glanced back at her lover who stared wide-eyed at Lincoln, like I was holding a writhing snake.

"That's the same kid, right, Mr. Pope?"

I was nearly over the moon with joy. Someone else noticed; I wasn't going cuckoo in the head.

Then Vicky went and shattered that notion. "Hun, if you're going a little soft in the head, we might need to get you some help... insisting a two-year-old is your grandson."

Shaking my head quickly, I reaffirmed that this kid was in fact Lincoln, that it was some kind of genetic thing. No idea if it was true, but I needed to leave him with someone I could trust fast, at least until I could figure out just what was making most of my friends and neighbors soft in the head.

I held him out to Vicky. "How long have you been serving me breakfast? Please, just trust me on this one."

Vicky looked in my eyes and I stared back with as much grit and honesty as I could muster, hoping, praying that she could see that I was serious.

The pretty blonde waitress let out a long-suffering sigh. "I can see Sammie Jo's face. I know you aren't lying, Grady, but damn if this ain't all manner of weird."

"You have no idea." I replied deadpan, handing my grandson to her.

I drove faster than I should have on the way home. Even if I was in a hurry, I pushed the envelope of the speed limits on the pine-enshrouded back roads. The dust was kicking up something fierce as I flew down the drive to my house.

The old police cruiser and Otis Porter were waiting for me.

I didn't bother slowing down. He had already seen me and there would have been no real purpose to pretending that I wasn't breaking the law.

Otis kicked the dirt as I locked the truck. "Could cite you for that speed, Grady."

"You never have before," I replied.

We shook hands and Otis sighed heavily. "Beau never made it home. Can't find his truck, it's like he just vanished."

My temper flared. "You think I had something to do with it? Is that why you're out here, Otis?"

Otis held up his hands. "Jesus, Grady, I've known you since we were in grade school. You don't have a murderous bone in you unless the Cowboys lose on Sundays. I just wanted to know if you'd seen him."

He was suspicious of me; I could tell it from his wide eyes that looked like they were seeing me for the first time. I glanced at the pistol on his hip and wondered if I could snatch it and blow his brains out before he had the chance to react.

What the hell was I thinking?

I stood back and apologized to my friend. The migraine had returned, splitting my brain right down the middle. My vision went sideways, and I staggered. Otis caught me easily and patted my back.

"Whoa man, whoa… what's wrong?"

"Migraine…" I managed to gasp out as the Sheriff hauled me into my own home and sat me down in my chair.

Otis was rummaging around in the kitchen. I could hear the drawers opening up and silverware being flung everywhere. "Where is your damn medicine cabinet?"

I shook my head and gestured back towards the bedroom "Bathroom." I gritted my teeth. "Second drawer."

My friend headed deeper into the house. I heard him call out faintly, "Where's Lincoln?"

I groaned in response, shutting my eyes. The splitting axe in my mind was strong and I felt Otis hands under my head. "Open up, bud."

I obeyed, and I felt the dry taste of pills on my tongue and a glass being lifted to my lips. The cool water trickled and carried the pills down my throat.

I couldn't tell if the medicine actually helped, but the heavy sense of happiness that had flooded through me was gone replaced by the hot and sweltering knowledge of grief and fear that had become my world.

"Lincoln is with Vicky."

"The waitress?"

I nodded and explained to Otis exactly why I had brought Lincoln to her. By the end of it, Otis looked pale enough to be a close relative of my grandson.

"You got booze? I need a drink."

I chuckled darkly. "Aren't you not supposed to drink on the job?"

"Fuck that, with what you're telling me I want to retire and leave all this in the rearview. I'm entitled to a damn drink."

I licked my lips and smiled. "You aren't wrong. Booze is above the refrigerator."

Otis brought back two glasses and we both nursed singles of bourbon that had been ruminating for a few years. Neither of us said anything as we stared at the ice cubes rattling around inside the glass.

It couldn't have been more than fifteen minutes; I checked my watch and the minute hand had barely ticked past 1:16.

"You don't think it's damn peculiar that the boy grew like he was eating super veggies?"

Otis didn't have to point it out to me, but I was more surprised by how my reactions came and went to it. Two days ago I had been ready to strangle him in the crib when I had seen the growth spurt, then that look from those big black eyes and I felt nothing but affection for the boy. Alternating anger and love, a mental war that confused me all to hell. I had always been an assertive man, and wishy-washy people had always been a pet peeve that I had eagerly scorned whenever the subject came up. Couldn't believe I was acting the same.

"And I've talked to Sheriff Schaefer down in Mooringsport a few times. Hubers pay him a pretty penny to look the other way. he's never mentioned a Savant Huber."

Maybe I had suspected that the man was making it up, but I wasn't a cop, didn't have the slightest clue how people came up with aliases or identities other than straight up lying.

Otis sighed and leaned back in his chair, scratching at his neck and taking another sip of the bourbon. "There was that story from when we were kids about Barnie Huber's eldest daughter, what was her name… you remember?"

I had remembered a few Hubers from Otis and me's grade school, but it had been over forty years and I couldn't recall the girl he was talking about.

"Holly Huber, that was her… God, she was a knock out."

I nodded in agreement. The memory came back strong: long blonde hair and cut off shorts that had left many a preteen boy drooling.

"Yeah, yeah I remember her now. God, my imagination ran wild with her when I was kid…"

Otis clacked his glass against mine and both of us smiled at the memory.

"Better than a Playboy." Otis smiled before that grin disappeared and he bottomed out the bourbon. "Well Holly went missing… supposedly met a guy and ran off… sound familiar?"

I bottomed out my own glass in response. "You think that Savant Huber is her kid?"

"Maybe. If he isn't then her disappearing just like…" He didn't finish and he ran his finger around the inside of the glass. "It's a helluva coincidence is all that I'm saying."

The thought was sobering, and suddenly the warm liquid coursing through me did nothing.

"I've got an alligator to hunt."

Otis looked like I had just hit him over the head as he stood up. "You can't be serious?"

"It's a man-eater and there is money involved. You bet your ass I'm serious."

Otis transformed from my friend into the grim manifestation of law enforcement that I had spent my life avoiding in the backwoods and bayous. "Grady, something is seriously wrong here, and if you can't see that then you're a fucking idiot…"

My temper flared up. "What do you want me to do Otis? I'm fucking alone! My daughter is dead, my wife is dead, and that boy is all I have left!"

The tears welled in my eyes. I was desperate, and in my heart I knew that Lincoln was at the center of something terrible, knew that something had been whispering for me to act like nothing was wrong with him.

Otis never wavered. He let me continue unabated. "I can't just... I can't..." Even my excuses rang hollow to my ears.

A smooth Cajun accent answered me. "Can't turn your back on your family."

Luc was standing in my doorway, his lips drawn into a thin line. "Hello, Sheriff. Good to see you."

Otis paled as he saw the resemblance. "You aren't—"

"That I am, here to tell you that there's bad whispers coming out of the river."

CHAPTER FOURTEEN

WE FOLLOWED LUC DOWN TO the boathouse and the river's edge.

"How come you didn't tell me that a Robichaude was back?" Otis hissed at me.

"Just found out myself. Why, scared?"

Otis looked taken aback, his cheeks deepening into a dark red, the ancient shame that he had allowed a lynch mob to escape justice under his watch.

"Worried for the bastards who actually did it."

My cheeks were hot and still wet. I hadn't bothered to wipe them. I was embarrassed letting my weakness show… now I was angry. Angry at the world, angry at God, my friends, everything…

Luc walked out into the shallows, his boots caked with the mud and grime. He gestured for us to follow suit.

Otis looked at the water and then his sweat-stained uniform. "Shit."

I walked out into the water without hesitation, letting the muddy water wash me clean from the damn sentiment and feeling towards anything, transforming me back into the cold bastard that Renee had accused me of being on her death bed.

My wife had a point. I had written off my daughter easily enough after she had left. I wouldn't claim any kind who betrayed her father for some lowlife.

"Alright, Mr. Robichaude, I'm sorry but I'm going to need some explanation about what the fuck this is!" Otis hadn't moved from his spot on the shore. He eyed the water, no doubt looking for snakes.

"You want to find your deputy sheriff? He's out there." Luc pointed to the middle of the channel with a dead certainty that shriveled up my anger and sent chill bumps racing, suddenly aware of how cold the water was and wanting to back out.

Otis paled, all embarrassment forgotten and reluctantly began stripping down until his brown slacks were the only thing left. A heart surgery scar and a nest of white hair crisscrossed his chest and a bit of a spare tire that I could relate too wiggled as he waded out to join us, looking like he would rather be doing anything else.

"Stay close to me, the things that we are about to parley with… well they don't really take too kindly to us."

I shook my head, nearly laughing. "Luc, you're a good showman for sure but let's be honest: the whole voodoo thing was just hearsay, your family were just normal folks… you don't have to play it up for us."

Luc's look stopped me cold as he cracked a cold smile. "You think that, Grady Pope?"

Otis put a hand on my shoulder to steady himself and I nearly jumped out of my skin at his touch. He looked scared... I had never seen him like this.

Hell, I hadn't been this frightened since I had discovered Luc's family.

Luc was whispering. Otis and I stood back, chills racing up our spines as something subtle weaved its way through the air.

Luc produced a small red pouch from the folds of his jacket and loosened the string, though keeping it bound. The cloth came apart and a smattering of dust and things too quick for me to make out tumbled into the river as Luc glared silently at the murk and mud.

There was a splash off to our right, a wake moving towards us, tell-tale signs of something massive moving under the water.

"Grady, Sheriff... I need you both to unburden your minds, and for your sake as well as mine, don't panic." Luc spoke calmly as his eyes fixed on the water in front of him. His hand twitched even though he tried to hide it.

"The hell, boy?" Otis spoke incredulously, like he couldn't believe what he was hearing, like it was some sort of grand joke that he wasn't in on.

"Your mind is going to be struggling to handle what it sees. You're going to want to run screaming. But I implore you both, stand your ground..."

Otis splashed forward in the water, striding past me as he fixed his best authority face. "Alright, this mystic shit stops now. I have a missing person, a man-eater, and don't have time—"

We never heard the log as it came flying through the air and landed with a hulking splash between Otis and Luc. The Sheriff screamed and fell backwards into the water then flailed, trying to find his feet. I hoisted him up and both of us stared at the massive piece of floating wood. I thought I could see Luc begin to sweat.

"Please, Sheriff, Grady, be silent and don't move."

Maybe it was the earnestness in his voice or my fear at what was swimming around us, but I bit down hard on my tongue and waited. The cold clamor of terror raced down my spine as I stood waist deep in the river and looked around me.

Luc said something that I couldn't make out, and there was a temporary stillness that descended on the world. My breathing was sharp, and I could make out each individual wheeze and chatter of my teeth in the frigid water. The spring sun was blistering, but it did nothing to prevent the chill creeping across my body.

I could hear Otis' ragged breathing as he attempted to keep himself in check, probably wondering like I was if the rumors were true about the Robichaudes and their strange proclivities.

Something brushed against my leg and I stiffened; it was smooth and reminded me of the gelatin desserts that Renee used to make me. I blinked quickly and saw the water roiling and Luc glancing intently around us.

CATFISH IN THE CRADLE

"Don't move, Grady!"

Luc's voice carried authority, and I kept both eyes riveted forward on him. I heard multiple splashes around me, and each one was like a bullet shooting through my senses. After every muffled splash I flinched until I was practically shaking.

My instincts were screaming at me to run. I had been around enough large predators to know when I was outclassed… whatever it was behind me could tear us limb from limb. It was just a feeling but one that I knew beyond a shadow of a doubt was fact.

The sound of dripping water echoed directly behind me, and beyond my gaze I felt something to my immediate right stand tall out of the water.

There was something to be said for that feeling of being watched or that someone was standing behind you. Ancient instincts and feelings left over from when caveman huddled around fires and prayed to whatever heathen god would listen that they wouldn't be the next thing screaming in the dead of night as they choked on their own blood.

That's how I felt now with whatever was standing next to me.

There was an odd sucking noise and then a deep warbling.

I felt a deep-seated terror fill my soul and I struggled not to run or collapse into the water.

Luc replied in the same loathsome tongue consonants and grunts combining into something unintelligible. It sounded so wrong coming from a man's lips, like it should have set his mouth aflame and made his gums bleed.

The smell hit me like a tidal wave, a powerful musk of primordial strength that made me want to cover my nose to hide the scent, only for it to snake up my nostrils and infect every inch of me. Nausea flooded me, and I tried not to vomit as I struggled to keep my feet planted firmly in the mud under me.

"Robichaude, what the hell is this? What's going—" Otis voice wavered to my left, like he had regressed forty years into a child withering under his father's glare.

"*Quiet!*" Luc hissed, and I heard Otis give out a small yelp. I could hear his breathing becoming rapid and I was afraid that his years of pigging out on greasy burgers and chain smoking were about to catch up with him.

Whatever it was that had stood up from the water leaned close to me. A hot breath hit my face and it smelled like old blood and heavy mud. More croaking speech that Luc returned, and I suddenly felt a grip like iron close around my throat. It was loathsome, like rubber and snakeskin mixed together; I could smell the rot underneath the sharp nails that pinched into my skin.

I gurgled beneath the grip but kept my eyes firmly shut. Luc spoke fast and the thing holding me answered. Whatever conversation they were having wasn't pleasant.

"Grady?" Otis called. He was terrified. Hell I didn't blame him. "Oh… my… God…"

I knew before he began screaming that he had turned to look.

There was a gunshot, and the repulsive hand left my throat in a flash. I kept my eyes facing forward and my feet planted as Luc screamed something that I couldn't hear over the sound of Otis's terrified howls, raising a hand and making the sign of the cross through the air. Gurgling roars like drowning lions echoed around me, and I heard Otis' screaming become a gurgle that faded away just as quick.

It was over; the echoing splashes and roars fading into the normal birdcalls and distant boat engines.

Luc panted, wandering over to shake my shoulder. "It's... okay, Grady." His voice quivered, and when I looked close I could see the fresh tears that he was trying to hide as he looked helplessly at me. "I told him not to panic."

Otis was gone, his spot in the water still calming down from whatever had come up from the river.

"Where is he..." I managed to grunt out. I wanted to scratch the skin off my neck, I could still feel the awful touch.

"They've taken him down to the Cradle. I..." Luc took a shuddering sigh as he grasped my shoulders. "He didn't listen."

There was a groan that echoed through the water, and the tail end of Chevy pickup suddenly bobbed to the surface in the center of the river.

I stared with morbid curiosity as I tried to make sense of what my world had become. There was no damn sense, just shit that would have made a braver man lose himself.

I recognized that truck. It was Beau Caldwell's. The metal was covered in mud and silt, green algae suckled over the chassis and inside the tire groove. The paint had been scratched by drifting debris, and the cab had flooded.

I could see the barest outline of a hand behind the glass, a crawdad chewing happily on the bloated extremities.

"How—" I stammered it out and Luc looked grimly as Beau Caldwell's swollen face floated past the window, eyeballs rolled up and skin hellishly purple. The crawdads that had found their way into the truck at the bottom of the river snipped at the stringy and rotten strands of his exposed neck.

The bottom feeders feasted, and I realized that Beau Caldwell had been snapped in two before his head had been ripped off.

My stomach churned, and I reached out for something to support me and found Luc's shoulder waiting. My vision was swirling, and darkness spun at the edges.

Luc's voice drifted into my ear. "Come on, Grady, I'll get you fixed up… then we'll talk."

I came to in a wooden chair that didn't recline. My back hurt terribly.

Luc had redecorated the inside of Cy's cabin. Bottles full of plants and spices that I couldn't identify littered the exposed shelves while the furniture all looked homemade, carved lovingly with intricate designs whose meaning went over my head. I sniffed and caught the scent of honey, a crisp warm smell mixed with a hint of nature. Luc was at his kitchen counter, staring intently at a teakettle that was beginning to steam under a warm flame from the stove. Bones, powders, and odd items that made me think of something exotic decorated virtually every space that was available. I shifted in my chair, looking around at everything and trying to hide the fear that was beginning to jump through me.

"I like to handmake things. Patience is a virtue when you do what I do." Luc said softly as he poured the tea into matching chipped green cups and walked over, handing one to me. "Drink up, you'll feel better."

I sniffed it and the aroma was pleasant, but I still eyed it warily "Is this…" I felt incredibly stupid saying the next words. "Magic tea?"

To his credit Luc didn't laugh. "No, Mr. Pope, just some herbal tea like Mom used to make. It'll take the edge off."

I still wasn't entirely convinced, but I began sipping the concoction slowly. it washed down my throat and I felt a sense of peace and calm come over me.

Otis…

My hand clenched around the cup hard enough for the warmth to seep in and sear my skin. There would be a small blister when it was over, but that paled in comparison to the pain I felt.

"What… the hell… happened to him?" I enunciated every word, letting my young friend know that I wasn't fucking around. I needed answers: about Lincoln, about Otis, about every piece of weird shit that had permeated my life since Sammie Jo had reappeared on my dock.

"You sure you want to know?" Luc walked around the living room, my eyes following every step as he examined the various jars and rearranged them, his hands trailing down the small chicken bones he had strung from the ceiling. "Once you know, Mr. Pope, there is no going back."

"Cut the shit and tell me."

Luc smiled with no humor. "My family was around for a long time, Mr. Pope. Came down and settled in the 1700s, if you believe old Grandpappy's tales. From there our kin spread all over Texas and Louisiana: hoodoo workers, voodoo priests, traiteurs. Everyone had an inclination towards the more spiritual side of things."

My hands were shaking as I tried to sip on the tea. The rumors were true: he and his had practiced black magic.

Maybe he could see the look in my eyes or maybe the tensing of my shoulders. Either way he swiftly defended himself. "It isn't evil, Grady Pope. I don't traffic with the Devil or any other kind of witchcraft. Magic, hoodoo, everything is all about intent and entreating the right things."

I was feeling guilty that I had saved this man when he was just a boy. My anger flared, and I decided to stab at him where it really hurt. "None of that saved your family though, did it?"

That easy-going smile disappeared and suddenly I felt very alone and very powerless before the Cajun as his fist clenched. There was a sudden growling, and I froze in my seat.

A monster emerged from the garage. It was the biggest dog I had ever seen, all muscle and white fur with teeth like daggers.

"There you are, Mojo," Luc said simply, and the dog ceased growling at me and padded over to his master who proceeded to scratch behind his ears.

"You're a good man, Mr. Pope, and I respect you. I owe you my life, but don't speak of my parents in that way."

The massive dog leaned into him and I gulped down the rest of my tea, trying to hide that the Cajun man intimidated me.

"What you do in this world comes back sevenfold. The folks who murdered my kin will pay, of this I swear to you."

Luc sipped from his own cup of tea and licked his lips afterward, looking out towards the river. "That being said, I don't reckon I'll be taking up that grudge until we solve the Deep Folk's grievance."

Deep Folk. I had never heard the phrase before, but I figured that he must have been talking about whatever it was that had taken Otis and put its ghastly hand around me.

"There are old things in this world, Mr. Pope, things that people aren't equipped or don't want to see. They came up from the Atlantic. You see my family entreated them here, made pacts and promises. This was before they blew up the Great Raft and the lake lowered; that's where it all started…"

Luc shuddered as his eyes closed. It scared me to see his own hand trembling, the tea bouncing up and running down his hand. Mojo licked his other hand as Luc gritted his teeth. "I had only seen them once before today, back when I was a boy and their chieftain came to entreat with my father. The Deep Folk don't like the light of day or interacting with humans. But down under the lake, down in the Cradle, they feast and mate and kill…"

He spoke with conviction, with fear, and with a certainty that every word that he was speaking was true. I was almost afraid of the answer, but I asked the question that had come to my mind since the beginning.

"What are they?"

"The First Tribe, Primordial Rulers, the Bishop Fish, Dagon… Man has called them many things over the countless millennia. There is no word in our language for what they call themselves in their tongue."

Luc turned and began rummaging through an old drawer until he removed a book that looked like it had seen the better part of a few centuries. "This is *The Charor Psalms*, written in a language long dead but handed down through the centuries and teachable, if you know where to learn."

The book landed heavily in front of me, the ancient hide cover flipping open ancient parchment flipping. Words written in diagonal and spiraling text were scrawled across the page, hard angles and periodic dots. It looked like nothing I had ever seen and nearly hurt my eyes to look at.

"Don't stare at it too long. It does nasty things to the head if you don't properly prepare. But you want to know about the Deep Folk? Turn the page."

Luc patted me on the shoulder as he passed, heading into the kitchen. Out of the corner of my eye I saw him remove a bottle of Pernod and begin pouring himself a glass.

I flipped the page in front of me.

There was a drawing on the next page, detailed to the point it could have been a photograph. The image was like a man but with a square head, sharp blocky teeth like a guillotine's blade, black eyes as deep as an ocean, pallid brown and green skin that spoke of savage muscle, with webbed hands and feet that ended in hooked claws that the artist depicted dripping in blood. A bloated belly and a monstrous member hanging between its legs completed the image of this monstrous cross between fish and man.

My mind swirled... I thought I was going to be sick.

Luc gently closed the book and set a glass of Pernod into my hand, advising me to drink.

"Imagine seeing one in person. If you don't come properly prepared, you'll be vomiting for a week." He whispered a few words and my nausea began to disappear. "These are the things that you heard speaking and that took Otis."

"Why?" I managed to choke out, and my friend tapped the book in front of me. "The Deep Folk know the ins and outs of unspeakable and ancient rites that I don't. The book says they can mask themselves to our minds, make us see what's not there or worse: overwhelm the senses."

"No, *why* did they take Otis?"

Luc swallowed all of his Pernod in one go and began pouring himself another one before setting his glass on the floor and drinking straight from the bottle. "I tried to reason with them, let them know that you watched over Lincoln and that Otis was a sworn protector of Uncertain... I thought together we could make a new pact with them."

Another swig. Mojo appeared by his side, whining softly, and Luc reached down to scratch his ears. "But it's pointless. They've all gone mad, insane in the mainframe, fucking frenzying to mate with anything that they can get their hands on." Luc chuckled mirthlessly. "At least I compelled them to bring back the deputy's body."

I leaned back in my chair, just staring at the wall, trying to wrap my mind around all of this and realizing that I had hopped, skipped, and fallen straight down the fucking rabbit hole.

It was all crazy and it was all true.

I had never been keen to the existence of the supernatural or anything so crass. Even God in church on Sunday was more abstract.

Magic and fish monsters, fucking crazy.

Lincoln…

"You said something about guarding my grandson… why would they even care?"

Luc sighed and took another swig of the bottle, a deep one, then pointed a crooked finger at my chest. "Now we come to the crux of it. They've done put a powerful working on your mind."

I snorted, my subconscious desperately hoping that it was a joke and Luc's grim features letting me know it was anything but.

"How could they… never even caught a glimpse of them when they came up…" I sounded like a school kid whining to the teacher about his poor grades. I was pushing sixty and the thought sickened me to my core.

"It's been laid on you from the start. Once you laid eyes on your grandson it was laid on you."

I knew what he was implying. The realization had already dawned on me, but I began shaking my head, refusing to believe it.

"I whipped up a little something that I thought might help clear the cobwebs in your head." He produced a small red bag tied with a cord and slipped it over my neck before

CATFISH IN THE CRADLE

I could protest.

The floodgates opened and the weight I had been feeling on my life dried up. Lincoln's birth came first, but it wasn't a newborn covered in steaming afterbirth and blood but a fish-shaped abomination that squalled deep warbling cries at me.

"They come out of the womb fully ready to subjugate the uninitiated." I heard Luc say faintly.

More of the horrid sight of that squalling thing before he was two years old and standing in front of me, the blocky shape of his head already formed and the beginnings of muscle beginning to show on his frame. The clothes I had given him were mildewed and frayed, and with a small warbling gurgle he grinned.

"G'mpa!"

I screamed and tore myself out of the memory, panting hard before I realized the full extent of what was happening. I broke down into sobs at the confirmation that my grandson, my last flesh and blood, wasn't my flesh and blood at all.

Should have taken my rifle and ended it, put a bullet right through my brain and slipped off to Hell. Would have been better that way.

Luc patted my back and didn't say anything until the tears had run their course and I sat in silence, unable to speak or say much of anything.

"It's my family's fault, you know." Luc sounded mournful. "They lured them up from the Gulf with promises, that this place would be their home, that no harm would come to it… so they swore."

Luc pulled up a chair and sat across from me. Mojo laid his head down in his lap and his owner stroked the massive white head. "Then came the destruction of the Great Raft, then the oil wells in the big lake, and the ammunition plant. The Deep Folk ignored it for as long as they could, content that my kinfolk were working their art against the powers that be."

He was lost in a memory now, his eyes looking a someplace distant that I couldn't see. "That ammunition plant was the end of everything for us. It was the mercury you see, dripped right down into the Cradle and drove all of them mad. They used to peaceful, intelligent. Now look at them: ignorant savages worshiping a toxin as a god." It was like he was hardly aware of me now, lost in the ennui of old memories and times long past.

"Stunted their children when they had them, wretched things that had to be put down as soon as they came slithering out of the womb. That's why they started abducting people with the help of everyone they whammied. Even then, that just produces stunted things out of some inbred nightmare."

He sighed, and for a moment he didn't look like a young man barely hitting his prime but an old soldier that had seen too much and walked away with even more pain.

"My dad tried to get it shut down several times." Luc snorted and raised a middle finger towards the sky. "But there ain't no fighting city hall, is there?"

He was in full form now spitting each word with venom at no one in particular before shrinking in his chair, patting his dog on the head and joining me in my blank stare, both of us lapsing into silence.

Maybe ten minutes passed with only muffled bird song supplying noise.

"I'm going to have to kill Lincoln, aren't I?" My voice was calm, quiet, devoid of hope.

Luc looked up at me and slowly shook his head. "No. That would just end whatever restraint they have. His father would declare open war. Uncertain, Mooringsport, Ferry Lake… they'd kill everyone."

Father…

The word roused me from my morbid thoughts; my anger lifted its head and smelled blood. Subconsciously I knew that one of them had to have been the boy's father, but seeing that Luc Robichaude knew which one of these blasphemous monsters it was… that gave me a terrible hope.

"You can point out Lincoln's father? You know which one he is?"

Luc nodded his head, seeing the terrible gleam in my eye. "Don't even think about it, Mr. Pope. They're stronger and faster than any man. He'd tear you apart before you could get a shot off."

I didn't protest. I now knew that the thing was closer than I thought it had been. Just had to wait for the opportunity to kill it.

"Your grandson is the first pure born they've had in a long time. That's why they want him so bad. He ain't deformed or mixed up in the head like the rest. He's full, one hundred percent primal monster."

I took this in with the same measure I took all of the rest, wondering how in the world I was ever going to come back from this with my sanity intact.

"He isn't ready to live down there with them yet, no gills you see." The Cajun hoodoo man made double lines across his neck like a mocking execution. "Make no mistake though: they're coming, which is why I need you to go back down to your house and bring Lincoln here. They've been working heavy on you to raise him until he's ready to come down to the Cradle, and I've been doing my damned hardest to break it, but my methods work better up close."

I clutched the bag that Luc had slipped around my neck. "I don't know if I can look at him. I just... he's a fucking monster."

"He's also your blood. No matter what you say or where he comes from, he's your kin and he's human enough to love you at least for a little while more."

I sighed and wobbled to my feet, feeling every ache and pain that had accrued in my fifty-eight years. "You're going to have to be my voice of reason when we pick him up, Robichaude. He's not human and he killed my baby girl just by being born. The little bastard can hang for all I care." I stabbed a finger at Luc, my anger realized and on full display. "If you want him you can have him, but he ain't no kin of mine."

The Cajun should have thought better of it before he worked his hoodoo and made me see the truth of things; I wasn't under some fish fucker's mind whammy now. I saw the truth and there was no love in it.

Luc seemed to ignore everything I said as his face paled. "Pick him up?"

That caused a bit of confusion on my part. Usually people responded to a cuss filled tirade trying to reason with me. "Yeah, I left him with Victoria Barnes at her place…"

Luc turned before I even finished talking and began gathering a few things and muttering under his breath.

"What is it?"

The Cajun ignored me, rummaging around in his drawers and bottles. "High John the Conqueror Root, Silver Dime, Paper, Bible…" The list made absolutely no sense to me and it was only when I grabbed his shoulder that Luc seemed to snap out of whatever fugue he was in and look at me.

I had never seen him look afraid until now.

"Grab your gun Mr. Pope. You've handed the first Deep Folk pure blood born in twenty years over to the people that seduced your daughter away from you."

CHAPTER FIFTEEN

THE TRUCK BOUNCED OVER THE long road. It was an older model Dodge from the seventies; the paint had been beat all to hell and the A/C didn't work, but Luc said that it was the little things that made this truck special. His father Jean Phillipe Robichaude had smoked cigars exclusively and had often snuck out to sneak a puff in the cab when his mother Felicite caught him in the house. On their way to church one Sunday, his youngest brother Leon had wedged a toy horse in the alcove on the inside door and it wouldn't come out. His older brother Cyprien had ridden in the bed and had drawn little designs on the inside of the metal. His sister Bastienne, a few cousins and other relatives… all of them had somehow made their mark on that truck. Despite the passage of years and toll it had taken, Luc had endeavored to keep it running.

I could smell the ancient hints of burning leaves and tobacco stains that spoke of Jean Phillipe's old habits. It was all trying to distract me from the facts Luc had told me.

Sometime ago after the Robichaudes had failed to protect their home, the Deep Folk had made a new pact. Certain citizens of our beloved little community had discovered the fishmen. They were compelled into something monstrous: the great treasures the river had swallowed were offered up to people who would see fit to sacrifice their sons, daughters, and wives in return. Not death—no, that would have been a mercy. They were taken down to the Cradle, never to be seen again.

I always thought that the official report of the Klan killing Luc's family had been convenient. Sketchy even back then, but with the knowledge that there was a damn cult worshiping rapist fishmen, I had my doubts. Luc shared my sentiment.

"My cousin Guy brought me back a few years ago, helped me go back to the old homestead and recover what little magic that hadn't been destroyed. Caught one of them and 'persuaded' it to talk."

His grip on the wheel tightened and I thought I felt the truck pick up speed. "Half these people are probably whammied so hard they don't know how much time has passed. They're trying to gaslight you hard, Grady."

I didn't have time to ask any more questions as we tore down Vicky's driveway and came to rest before the house. Her home didn't look as bright and hopeful as it had earlier that morning. I noticed everything that I had previously ignored: pieces of wood that the termites had gotten to, the chipped brick, crow droppings all over the roof. Filth covering the veneer of humbleness.

"There is a way in around back."

Luc nodded, and I loaded the revolver I had brought with me. I slung the rifle over my shoulder and offered him my old 12 gauge, but he refused, pointing to the Bible in his jacket pocket. "This is powerful protection and my weapons aren't as obvious."

I hadn't seen any fireballs or seas parting yet, but hell, the fish people had made a believer out of me.

There was no way that they hadn't heard the truck's engine, but I wasn't worried. I wanted them to know I was here.

Wanted them to be afraid.

I admit that is desperate logic, but it gave me peace and made me feel braver than I actually felt. Couldn't believe it, wouldn't believe it. Vicky and Gideon wouldn't betray me—they had been just as shocked at Lincoln's appearance as I had been.

"How do you know they weren't feeding you what you wanted to hear?"

Luc and I crept around the side of the house and I listened, trying to discern any noise coming from inside but hearing nothing but silence. We hit the brick wall of on the left side of the house and I strained on my tiptoes to look in the old window nearest me. Moisture had worked its way in between the glass panes over the years and had smudged the glass into a blurry tapestry that my old eyes had trouble seeing through.

From what I could see, the house was dark and empty.

Distantly I heard vague cheers and immediately knew where they were.

I tore across the lawn, heading straight for tree line and the woods; Luc was hot on my heels, trusting my judgment.

I could see Arnold Kizer and his wife with their backs to me huddled around Lincoln who drank deeply from an identical well that rested behind the parsonage. Couldn't see hide nor hair of Vicky.

"*Hey, hey!*" I screamed as loud as I could and aimed the shotgun.

I heard Luc whispering prayers behind me as Richard whirled around. His face was a mask of comfort, but it was just that… a mask. Beneath that smile that promised to help I could see the bulging throat and pointed teeth hidden behind the pearly whites.

"Be careful, Grady Pope. He's one of their half-breeds." I glanced at Luc who clutched one of the red bags he had made tightly in his hand. At the mention of his race, that kindly smile dropped from the pastor's face as his eyes dissolved in his head. The blue, comforting orbs trickled out of his face like runny egg yolk, silvery mercury splattering against the grass. They were replaced by black orbs so dark they might as well have been the deepest point of the ocean.

There was a popping sound; Arnold's teeth began falling out of his head in bloody spurts as the sharp fangs as thin as toothpicks forced their way through his flesh. His dark skin paled and became a sickly grey. It finished its perverse transformation into a thing that only barely resembled the man it had been imitating.

Jeanette fell to her knees and bowed low as Arnold patted the side of her head, fused flesh leaving wet streaks in her hair. A warbling flow of consonants and croaks assaulted my ears and I gritted my teeth. It was horrible to listen to, like its sires in the river. My ears felt like blood should have been pouring out of them.

"Don't know what the fuck you're saying, but I swear to God one wrong move and I'll be splattering caviar all over these trees." I meant it; my finger was twitching against the trigger guard.

"Grampa?" And just like that, everything became moot.

Lincoln was a young man now, maybe thirteen years old. The clothes I had given him were tatters on the pine needle floor. His looks favored his mother; I could see the light curve of her chin on his face. The fused skin between his toes and hands had grown; I could see the veins pulsing beneath the flesh. His nails also had grown, beginning to curve into the talons of his other kin.

"Grampa, don't hurt him... he and Miss Jeanette are helping me."

"Lincoln? Why don't you come over here?" Luc's cool cadence didn't do anything to assuage my fear as my grandson shook his head.

Dead skin peeled as his head and moved, revealing the dark muddy scales underneath it. "Can't do that sir... my family needs me."

The thing that had been Arnold Kizer croaked rhythmically, laughter no matter what language you spoke.

"You want to play with me?" I shoved the rifle towards the former preacher. "One more evil laugh and you'll be picking up brain matter."

"Grampa, please." Lincoln stepped between me and Arnold. "Savant tried to convince you earlier, but you weren't ready to let me go… he's told me the truth these past few hours about what I am."

My first instinct was to shoot him; his father was shining through those blank eyes and scales, his growth and slow transformation into a fucking freak… but his damn face… so much like his mother.

I cursed myself and my damn heart that ached never to be alone.

"Boy, your mom died because of these things and I can't promise you I'm ever going to forget that. But I'm your blood, not this… *thing*!" I spat the word at Arnold or whatever the hell this monster was in front of me.

Lincoln shook his head, arms raised. "Mom broke the rules; she had pledged herself to my father." My grandson looked genuinely sympathetic, hard to achieve when your teeth looked like they could have ripped the flesh off an alligator. "I don't expect you to understand… but Arnold has told me how the faith works, how happy the brides are. Just look at Jeanette!"

The preacher's wife nuzzled her head against the fishman's hijacked flesh, smiling contently.

"It's an honor to become a bride and this town's duty to provide them."

"Because they can't get it up for their own." Luc spoke with confidence, clutching the mojo bag in his hand tight. "They need you Lincoln, to continue this farce... this pact... you're the first since old days, but you have free will, don't have to do what they say you have to do."

My grandson looked at the Cajun warily. "They told me about you too... about your sister..."

Luc fell into silence, glaring at Lincoln. My grandson looked guilty as he glanced between us and the abomination.

I glared at the fish faced monstrosity standing close by with his brainwashed woman. "I'm going to give you one warning: get the hell away from my grandson, get back to whatever hell you swam out of and tell his Daddy that if he has a problem, he can come take it up with me!"

I didn't expect for it to answer back. "I tried to tell you Grady Pope... my master wants his... son." The words came rumbling from its repulsive throat and I sneered in reply.

"Well he can come and tell me himself."

The thing smiled "The log wasn't... enough?"

My blood ran cold and I pulled the trigger.

The rifle fired and a bright spout of red blood appeared and Lincoln screamed incoherently as Savant clutched its neck, gurgling. Jeanette screeched and rushed to the thing, holding it and rocking it gently.

Lincoln's eyes pooled with tears. "It could have been better Grampa, you don't understand!"

"Boy..."

Savant screeched and lunged towards me; I fumbled trying to chamber another round.

Only Luc's intervention saved me. Clutching the mojo bag tight he stepped forward, muttering prayers and sanctities. The fishman recoiled as Luc stepped forward. "I treat powers and principalities beyond even you."

Lincoln ran forward, trying to get his hands on the Cajun; I clocked him over the head with my rifle. He dropped like a stone bleeding from the blow.

Savant gargled an unearthly gargle before his free hand tightened around Jeanette's throat and scuttled back to the well. The flesh seemed to fall off of him with every step, the stone scraping great pallid chunks as he tossed himself backward into the well, dragging the woman with him.

There was a second of silence and then a distant splash. Luc and I both rushed to the edge of the well but could only see darkness and the faint echo of disturbed water.

CHAPTER SIXTEEN

LINCOLN STAYED UNCONSCIOUS FOR THE drive back to my home. I wanted to call the police, the Army, hell, the National Enquirer… we had proof literally tied up in my living room.

Luc had found himself at home in my bourbon and drank a triple. Apparently working magic had its tolls that I didn't even bother trying to understand.

"Army won't believe you, police will lock you up… treat Lincoln like he's got a skin condition, not like he's a half human spawn of a primordial race."

"Well what are you suggesting then, Luc? Me and you against the monsters? Regular jamboree, ain't it?"

The Cajun ignored me, continuing to nurse his glass. "The problem is we don't know who in this town are members of the Deep Church. Savant already proved that he's had sway over their minds."

"Can't you just put a whammy on them or something to find out who is in bed with the fish?"

Luc rotated his glass and gave me a look that made me feel like I had just added up to four and had come out with five instead. "It doesn't work like that."

I threw up my hands in exasperation and sank into my chair, reaching for the bottle of bourbon that Luc passed over willingly.

"Tell me, was there ever a real Arnold Kizer?"

Luc shook his head. "If there was, his innards have long been digested. That's the danger of them half human children… what conjuring they can do is put to terrible purpose."

He glanced over at Lincoln; I had put some old clothes on the boy that my belly had grown through rather than out of. He frowned as a long, stringy band of saliva fell from his mouth.

"Those skin suits are good for a time but come at the cost of a human's life." Luc coughed as the alcohol went down too quick. "Could walk around in someone else's flesh myself if I wanted to dirty up my soul."

I had grown up under my mother's strict teachings that trafficking in hoodoo, voodoo, and whatever else counted as witchcraft under the Lord's gaze, but I knew better than to voice my misgivings to the one man in the world that I could trust.

"Though there might be a way to find out." Luc sat up, staring out the window all of a sudden, a devil's grin played across his face. "Yes… yeah, that's how we will find out."

"Would you cut that theatrical bullshit and just speak plain?"

Luc rolled his eyes and pointed out to the river. "Where do you think a cult dedicated to fish people worships?"

As it turns out, they worshiped not that far away.

Night had fallen; we had both begun to prepare for our journey. Luc had spent the afternoon preparing workings and enchantments that he told me would be better if I didn't understand. To speak of the magic would deprive it of its power.

Mojo sat silently on the floor, his eyes glancing as his master burned candles inscribed with our names. Luc prayed to God for our safe passage in our journey, that his hands would guide us and envelop us in protection from the evils of the deep.

Prayers were all well and good, but I preferred a good rifle that didn't jam when it came down to it.

I had force fed Lincoln a cocktail that would keep him asleep for a few more hours. Luc snuffed out the candles when he finished his invocation and turned to me with a grave look.

"It's time."

I nodded and grabbed the keys to the boat. Luc leaned down and patted Mojo on the head. "Keep the boy here, buddy. Don't let anyone take him."

The dog chuffed and laid his head back down, eyeing Lincoln warily.

I took every gun that I owned; it wasn't like the dog was going to be taking up the revolver to shoot any intruders. I had made sure each was armed in full. An old duffel bag carried ammunition as I slung the shotgun and rifle over my shoulder, the revolver and Sig Sauer adorning hip holsters. I must have looked ridiculous, like some old west cowboy out to get the gold and the girl.

Luc and I walked out of the back door, heading down to the boathouse. We didn't speak to each other; nothing needed to be said as we loaded the boat and lowered it into the river.

We sped away down the channel and out into the main river. I flicked on safety lights as we flew across the water, dual red and green glows illuminated our faces as our wake disturbed the otherwise pristine river.

There were a few people out tonight, hunters most likely. We could see their boats nestled up small inlets and at the edge of creeks. I don't think they paid us much mind as we passed… just another couple of stiffs out to see if they could catch the man-eater and make a quick buck.

Couldn't know that an alligator with a taste for people was the least of their worries on this river.

A smattering of lake houses lined the right side of the river, fire pits and grills burning outside as families and friends took advantage of the warm spring weather. I had been to a few of those over the years, evenings of laughter and fun… hosted a few myself. Those were always the best evenings I remembered, shooting the breeze with Davis or Otis while the kids ran and played everywhere.

CATFISH IN THE CRADLE

That's the stuff that makes life worth living, when you find that little spot of peace in a busy and tough world. At the end of the day maybe that's why these monsters angered me: they had taken my daughter, soiled my grandson with their blood, and destroyed lives. Those peaceful and good times that I had enjoyed and at the back of my mind hoped to experience again would never come again.

I would make them pay.

We rocketed down Government Ditch heading for the big lake. Luc had his eyes closed doing some sort of mumbo jumbo to let him in on where we needed to go.

The salvinia and water parted before us and suddenly we left the trees behind and entered the big lake.

"To your left, Mr. Pope. That copse of trees over there… kill the lights."

I flicked a switch and the lights disappeared, drowning the both of us back into the darkness of the night. I throttled the motor down, letting the moonlight guide us until we reached the trees.

An old duck blind was nestled beneath the cypress, the rusty stilts keeping it from sliding headlong into the lake. Whoever had built it used Spanish moss and reeds to disguise the wood and metal. The ducks would never realize it was there. Hell, it was so well disguised that if Luc hadn't told me where it was I wouldn't have known it was there.

"Tie us off at the bottom. There should be a ladder."

There was a small platform of wooden planks that had seen the better part of years. I tested them, making sure they were sturdy before putting my full weight down. There were a few groans and the wood gave slightly but didn't break. Luc joined me on the platform and together we tied off the boat.

Like Luc had said, a small ladder allowed access to the blind and Luc disappeared up the rungs while I retrieved the duffel bag full of ammunition.

A pile of thatch and cypress hit the planks as Luc reappeared. "Let's be quick about camouflaging the boat. Don't know when this thing will happen."

I didn't think that we would be able to camouflage the 175 into anything natural looking but I went about trying the best I could, draping the cypress across tarps and off the side until the boat looked like I hadn't cleaned it in years. "If anyone comes close, that's not going to fool them."

Luc was already climbing back up into the blind. "Let's hope no one comes close then."

The inside of the blind had seen better days; there was a small table that had old stains, two shelves that had toppled to the floor and some old chairs.

"Why do you think they'll come out here?"

"This was my family's blind; I used to bring my little brother Leon out here. Good times..." He winced as the good memory transformed into a bad one. "The Deep Folk would meet Dad out here to when they had cause."

The both of us lapsed into silence after that; nothing more to say and afraid that our voices would carry.

It was a quiet night on the lake, humid air cloyed around us and the mosquitoes buzzed incessantly, little pinpricks of pain met with death as I smacked the festering insects one after another. It was miserable going and I worried that I would catch malaria, West Nile, or any of those new diseases that the news loved to harp on and on about.

There was a distant boat engine, probably fisherman speeding back towards Mooringsport, voices laughed from a distant lake house.

Everything was calm.

I began loading my weapons, remembering the old proverb about the calm before the storm. Luc was mostly silent, though I heard him whispering occasionally, picking up snippets of prayers and other words that I didn't understand. Hours passed slowly and the moon that had hung low under the trees now shone down brightly on the still waters.

There was a distant rumbling; it started small… thought it might have been a train somewhere in the deep woods.

The safety lights appeared like distant ghosts through the trees, the oranges, reds, and greens floating behind the forest as the boats appeared; three speed boats and a pontoon barge.

They came out of the channel that Luc and I had come from, back towards Uncertain. The occupants were shining gigantic spotlights that were bright enough to be miniature suns.

I ducked down. "If they shine those this way we're screwed."

Luc didn't look worried. "You would be surprised how unobservant people are when their minds are focused elsewhere."

I thought that was shit logic and I felt my heartbeat quicken as those grumbling boat motors grew closer and closer.

Lights shined through the small copse of trees, shadows playing merry havoc with my old eyes. I held my breath, worried that whoever manned this backwoods armada would hear the slightest noise.

The lights disappeared, and Luc gripped my shoulder in a tight grip and reassuring smile that I could see even in the dark.

The engines still sounded close when they were cut; silence except for the splashing wake echoing over the water. Luc and I stood up slowly, careful not to readjust our weight in case the ancient blind groaned in protest.

Maybe seventy yards away the boats had come to a rest; there were four splashes as cheap forty-pound anchors were tossed over the sides, sinking into the depths. I couldn't make out the occupants. I could hear a lot of voices, but with the wind and the still splashing wake I couldn't make out any that I recognized.

I saw the silhouette of a man step to the edge of the spotlight; every single beam had been focused on one spot in the water. Something was said that I couldn't make out, and then he raised something in his hand and hit it.

Clang… the toll of a bell deep and warbling echoed across the water… *clang*… again… *clang*… rhythmically over and over.

I had been to enough banks and restaurants to know a service bell when I saw one… just wasn't prepared for the unsettling notes that warped over the waves.

"My Mom told me stories… but I just… I never thought I would be chosen!" The voice was excited, sultry, could have easily sold sins to saints.

Or served my pancakes to me most mornings.

My heart sank, and my old bones rattled as my knees shook. I gripped the bar tight as Luc whispered in my ear, "Steady, old man."

I had known Vicky for a long time; she and Sammie Jo had been thick as thieves. The errant thought and suspicion creeped into my head; Luc said that my daughter had been led astray. Now I was sure that I had found the shepherd.

My grief flared, and my left hand sought my hunting rifle lying on the shelf in front of me. I was a decent marksman despite my years and it would be so easy. Little squeeze of the trigger, a temporary clap of thunder and a spray of blood sinking down into the muddy water.

Luc's hand gripped mine and he shook his head slowly. "There will be another time," he hissed. I tried to shrug him off and bring the weapon up to murder as many of these duplicitous stains as I could.

"Just wait, Grady... just wait." The tension between my arm and his strained my muscles as he met my glare with his own. The fight went out of me with a sigh and I released the weapon.

The bell tones had faded and even the voices on the boats had waned into silence.

I had swam a lot when I was younger. When you're a kid you aren't too worried about the river; there is no fear of anything because you think you're going to go on forever. Then you get older and you realize that feeling of something bigger brushing against the bottom of your foot might not be your imagination.

That's the same feeling I had sitting in that old duck blind.

Luc seemed to have the same feeling as I saw his knuckles whiten on the rusty scaffolding. In the spotlight I saw something brown rise slowly out of the water, straightening until its full body was on display.

It hurt my eyes and I gritted my teeth trying to keep the bile in my throat from erupting. "Say your prayers, Grady Pope," Luc whispered from beside me as he grasped the mojo bag and began muttering blessings and quoting psalms as he stared ahead. I mimicked the motion and immediately felt the bile drop in the back of my throat. That scratching against the white of my eyes faded; magic at its finest I suppose.

Hesitantly I glanced back out over the waters; my eyes didn't feel like they would boil from my head as I received my first glance of the Deep Folk, their oldest and most terrible form.

It was tall, maybe ten feet or more. The muscles rippled beneath an armor of scales that were occasionally cracked, revealing an oozing interior, dripping diseased-looking pus back into the river. Its face was a near copy of the one from the book; it jutted out from a gilled neck with a bone-like hardness ending in a guillotine-like plate of teeth inside that nearly beaked mouth. More dinosaur than fish to my eyes, its chest was bare except for a small sling that kept a satchel close to its hip that looked like it had been woven from moss. A wickedly tipped spear made from rock and marsh bark was held in its right hand, its fused flesh wrapped tightly around the shaft of wood.

More of them appeared from the waves, fairly uniform in appearance but for the coloring of their scales and the condition of their bodies.

It seemed like the Deep Folk wanted to put their best first. Stunted arms, superfluous eyes, missing teeth, smaller size… traits that didn't mesh with the powerful warriors that were illuminated in the spotlight.

"Now that's interesting…" Luc whispered as he stared at the parade of monsters. "Never seen all the deformed ones."

The ten-foot tall monstrosity that seemed to be their leader strode towards the pontoon barge, a small wake forming as his legs sloshed through the water.

The silhouette of a man knelt at the edge of the lights. "Great Vhi'octa, we praise you at the coming of the tide and the receding of the shore."

The voice added a double punch to my gut; it was gruff and course and could have only belonged to Earl Ray. Should have known that a man I suspected of beating his wife would be part of this.

"As we have bargained since the Robichaudes fell, we bring you the twin sacrifices under the moon… a gift of food and a gift of flesh."

A chorus of croaking warbles rent the air like the screeches of demonic warthogs, a frightening cacophony that definitely made folks turn over in their beds, moaning at unbidden nightmares.

The monsters were pleased.

There was a gasping grunt and then a pained scream. Another voice I recognized, but this one was afraid.

They dragged Gideon Whyte up from the back of the boat. Even from the distance and darkness I could tell that he was broken, dragged along by two men that I couldn't make out. The young man weakly raised his head and recoiled at the sight of the thing.

"Don't struggle, sugar. We serve the gods our bodies and are sacred to them." Vicky leaned down and kissed Gideon's head, causing him to struggle violently to get away from her lips. I thought I heard him try to say something only for it to come out in a mangled groan of pain.

Earl Ray stepped back into the bow as the two men dropped Gideon at the edge of the boat.

"I can't do nothing!" I hissed, reaching for the gun again.

"You have to. There is more at stake than one man's life… it'll be quick for him."

Fuck that.

I shrugged off his hand and grimly commanded him to get down to the boat. Then I started firing.

The first shot took the big one through the pectoral muscle, right over where a heart should be. There was a bright spray of silvery red blood and a rumbling groan of pain as the .308 tore through the loathsome thing's flesh and stained the water with its blood.

Never had some well-deserved payback felt so good.

There was a cacophony of croaking howls along with shouts from the cultists, wondering where the shot had come from.

I fired again, making sure to aim at one of the people on the boats. He went down in a spray of blood tumbling off the barge into the water. A few of the stunted deformed Deep Folk dove towards the new corpse and greedily sucked him under the waves.

Luc flung himself into the 175 and began throwing off the thatch and cypress we had barely disguised it with.

"Get to Gideon; get him out of here!" I roared as I fired another shot at one of the stunted Deep Folk now barreling through the water towards us.

"You're a brave fool, Grady Pope!" Luc shouted back as he keyed the engine and brought the boat motor to life.

I laughed merrily, I was going to die here and I knew it, but damn if my frustrations, my fear, everything that I had bottled through the past few days exploded in a fury of blood and scale.

Luc threw the boat in reverse just as one of the Deep Folk, a smaller one with a useless vestigial arm, reached the copse of trees. The Cajun threw a hand towards one of the trees and shouted something that I couldn't hear over the inhuman cries and boat engines. There was a splitting crack as one of the limbs shattered and fell. The creature looked up, momentarily confused before the jagged edge of the shattered branch pierced its bulbous black eye in a shower of blood. The beast howled in agony as it clawed at its eye with its single stumpy arm, diving back into the water and leaving a black smudge on top of the dark water.

I picked up the shotgun; no use firing a rifle when they were practically on top of me.

Luc sped away angling wide and heading for the boats that were shouting encouragement to their fiendish masters;

hopefully whatever juju he could muster was good enough protection since he hadn't bothered to take a weapon.

The first of the croaking and howling monstrosities reached the bottom of the blind and met with a 20-gauge shot. Its body fell back twitching as its deformed brothers fell on him with glee. The smoking shell went rolling across the floor as I pumped another one into the chamber.

A massive hand came shattering through the thatch and cypress, shelves splintering in two. I screamed as it closed around my arm and tugged. The grip made me lose my balance and fall through the hole, barely missing the docking planks and hitting the water hard.

I floundered, trying to get my bearings. The shotgun was lost, ripped from hands as the stunted and deformed fish people swarmed me.

Death should have been instantaneous, but instead it was like they were dragging me down to the bottom. My chest was burning desperate for air. I thought it was the moon glowing up above me, visible even through the murk. Then a shadow passed over it and I lost consciousness.

CHAPTER SEVENTEEN

I DIDN'T EXPECT TO WAKE up.

Nightmares filled my mind in that dark crevasse of sleep, images of malformed and disgusting Deep Folk bulging and discharging their filthy offspring. Lincoln strode among them, his head held high. His teeth had become pointed and his skin pulsing red scales. Part monster, but he still looked noticeably like a man; he would reach down and pluck one the squirming deformed infants from the pile of writhing newborns. Then he'd rip it open with those needle teeth, ignoring the plaintive mewling of the baby until it stopped squirming in his mouth.

A nightmare that played on repeat until I woke up in total blackness.

The earthen smell was almost overpowering. Something tickled my face and I recoiled, unable to see what it was. The texture in my trembling hand felt like roots.

I breathed out a sigh of relief and fell backward, feeling a hard mixture of dirt and stone. My clothes were wet. Couldn't have been out of the water for very long judging by the dampness, but in the darkness I had no idea where I was.

It was cold and underground, that much I could tell. But that could have been a dozen places that I knew of and probably hundreds that I didn't.

My memories came flooding back and I remembered what I had seen and what exactly had taken me into the water. I fumbled around in my pocket looking for anything: lose change, a .22 bullet I hadn't bothered to remove, and my lighter…

It might has well have been fire from God. I pulled it out of my pocket and flicked it, trying to get it to light and barely making a few sparks that failed to ignite the butane.

Fumbling in the darkness, those years of scout training coming back, I felt the wall behind me until I found stone. Vigorously I began striking the flint wheel against the stone, attempting to dry it off. My hands began to go numb, and by the time I thought it could work I could barely feel my extremities. My joints ached as I worked my fingers to try to get the blood flowing through them again, only flicking the lighter when I was sure I could ignite the flame. Damn age, catching up hard.

The butane ignited, and I laughed in triumph, the small flame chasing away the darkness.

I let my eyes adjust. It looked like I was in a small room or cave. Ancient wooden planks formed a door on the far side of the room. Roots dangled from overhead, tiny rivulets of water running off their dangling tendrils and down the soggy earthen wall.

I tried to stand up, wincing. My legs were sore and I reached out to steady myself and recoiled as my hand sunk into the muddy wall. My hand was caked with clay so black that it looked more like worm guts than wet soil; I wiped the chunks on my pants and tried to walk towards the door.

The floor sucked at my boots each step, making a disgusting squishing sound that reminded me of stepping on food that had fallen off my dinner table. I tried to ignore it, making my way to the door and pushing myself out into the darkness.

Nearly toppled into the abyss if I hadn't seen it drop off.

I was at the edge of a pit that ran as far as my meager light could see in both directions, a well-worn path full of loathsome foot prints, a heavy pattering like rainfall that I could barely make out from a tidal wave's worth of dripping water falling from above.

Left or right? Both sides looked nearly identical, thought I could make out the makings of another door off to my right. Fear gripped my chest as I began hesitantly trotting the path. *Pop... pop... pop...* my struggling steps sounded like one of those old nature documentaries where they over exaggerate the octopus sucker sounds.

Over the edge of the path and down in that vast darkness I thought I heard something roar. I froze in place and waited to see if some monster was coming to feast.

Nothing came of it, but the thought remained: why wasn't I dead?

It was a door that I had seen, a rotted slanted roof jutting out of the wall like the mud had swallowed it up. If there was anyone inside they should have been able to see the flickering glow of my lighter, but I looked inside nonetheless.

More of the wet, muddy floor, but there was a stone altar. I had spent enough time on my knees down at the front of the church to recognize what it was. Small humanlike idols and trinkets of gold adorned it, a crude carving of something I couldn't rightly describe… all misshapen and wrong.

My eyes itched to look at it and I had to turn away. I reflexively grabbed for the mojo bag around my neck and discovered that it was missing. Not surprising; these things hadn't seemed too keen on anything that Luc had peddled.

I took a step back, intending on continuing along the path when my foot slipped on a rock buried in the mud. Didn't even have time to yelp in surprise before I was tumbling over the edge.

I kept a tight grip on my lighter as I hit the water below, submerged in blackness that cloyed at my mouth and nostrils as I swam up gasping for air.

I couldn't see anything in the blackness, but I felt water splashing across my face like a rain shower. My feet weren't touching bottom and I closed my eyes, treading water and trying to calm my nerves. There was nothing there, just had to find an edge… the wall hadn't been that far away.

I swam to my right, reaching out for the wall and was rewarded when I felt my feet touch bottom. Relief flooded through me as I climbed out of the pool and laid on my side, trying to catch my breath. My heart felt like it was about to explode out of my chest.

It had just started thumping normally when I saw the blue glow. The light was coming from under the water in front of me. Twin points in the ever-present blackness. Didn't like when things came in twos; old memories of alligator eyes reflected in my spotlight came back and I tried to scramble quickly to my feet.

I was hurting. Hadn't had this much physical exertion in a long time, this alternative relief, fear, and adrenaline probably aging whatever years I had left out of me.

The thing came sloshing out of the water. It just kept coming, a ten-foot monstrosity that was hunched over and moved with a scraping limp. A gigantic wooden stick was held in its hand that it tapped against the mud.

This one wasn't like the rest. It didn't have scales as much as smooth skin. Its face was scarred a pair of whiskers hanging down from its cheeks, though one had been torn in half. Reminded me of the catfish I had hauled up from time to time.

The eyes though. I stared in fascinated horror at the twin things growing from them. Two twin worms were growing straight from its near useless eyes, glowing an almost neon blue.

The mud sucked at my foot as I stepped further to the left.

The creature growled low and began looking around, craning its head back and forth.

It was blind.

I kept virtually still, not daring to question my good fortune as the monstrosity sniffed the air, sharp webbed fingers scratching around its eyes.

My eyes were watering; the pain had started low behind my eyes and had grown to fever pitch. It felt like someone was scraping the back of them with a thorn bush.

I didn't blink, didn't move, and tried not to think as I gritted my teeth against the pain and tried to keep my mind from spiraling off into insanity. The pain was almost unbearable.

The Deep Folk waited, probably wondering if I was going to make a move. Then it grunted and began moving off. I watched as long as I could until it ducked into a crevasse and disappeared.

I fell to the ground, mud splattering against my knees as I desperately began splashing water in my eyes, trying to alleviate the burning sensation.

Couldn't let the light disappear…

I could still see the blue light shining but it was swiftly fading. I sprinted, barely making it to the rock entrance before the glowing light disappeared completely. My eyes were blurry, but I could still make out the shape of the revolting thing hunched and waddling down the passage.

I could feel warmth running down my cheeks and I dabbed at them, expecting to wipe away tears.

My vision may have been blurry and phosphorescent glow barely illuminating anything, but the dark smudges on my fingers weren't tears, my own covered my hands, I was bleeding from my eyes.

CATFISH IN THE CRADLE

I limped forward as quietly as I could, the sucking mud giving way to a pathway of stone.

From somewhere deep I heard something boom, like a deep pounding drum.

I froze behind the Deep Folk, maybe twenty feet, as it hastened its pace making a right turn at a fork in the tunnel.

For a minute I thought about drying out my lighter again but with how loud I had been earlier I was damn sure that the thing would hear me. Its sight may have been shot to shit, but I bet its hearing worked all too well.

I followed behind it, careful to make sure that my footfalls weren't making too much noise. It had quickened its pace, seemingly eager to answer the beat of the drums that were now pounding away deep in the bowels of this hell.

There were hollows and side caverns branching off the side of this tunnel, things I didn't bother to explore as I passed, my mind conjuring images of horrible things just waiting for me to step in their line of sight and become easy prey.

The tunnel began widening and another glow began to fill the tunnel, orange and red… fire. A roaring reached me that mixed in with the now steady beat of the drums.

The tunnel ended, and the creature walked out of it while I hid behind a pile of rocks in a small crevasse near the exit. The cavern was massive with jagged rocks and tidal pools of liquid mercury filled with glowing algae. Torches burned everywhere next to crude wooden cages and altars.

One rock more massive than the others jutted from the pool at the center of the cavern. It had been carved into a massive idol of a Deep Folk, chiseled in the likeness of its primordial glory. A waterfall of mercury oozed down from above, drowning the idol in its torrent and forming the pool at its feet. My vision might have been shot but I could definitely make out all the blood that was mixed in that silvery lagoon.

On ledges and alcoves around the cavern, Deep Folk beat drums. And on the floor, The fishmen were clustered beneath the idol, all of them waiting, larger fully-formed specimens at the front while their deformed brethren scampered and hissed behind them.

Men and women lay in a heap between the creatures writhing in the mercury, their stomachs grotesquely swollen in pregnancy.

Bile rose in the back of my throat and I fought to keep myself from vomiting. I shut my eyes tight... so many of these revolting things and then that... my mind couldn't take it anymore.

I rocked back and forth, knew I had to be in their home... the Cradle. There was no other explanation.

The birthing screams echoed in my head like Sammie Jo's own on repeat, complete with the squealing infant that came caterwauling from their wombs.

My mind told me not to, that I would I would never forget what I was about to see, that I would spend the rest of my life having sleepless nights screaming into the dark at what was at the bottom of the lake.

I looked. The men were dead, their bellies ripped open, lifeless eyes as wide as their mouths, that last scream of pain shadowed on their faces. The women were a mix.

CATFISH IN THE CRADLE

Some just looked tired and hollow ,others jubilant. The tall, fully-formed Deep Folk reached down and picked them up, carrying them away like a bride. Their deformed comrades fell upon the dead men with ravenous glee, bits of blood and sinew flying.

Under them, weaving in and out between their legs, were tadpole like monstrosities new to life and eager to feast on what their older brothers left behind.

This wasn't like Lincoln; these things weren't whole…

A mad chuckle escaped my lips… they were dying slow. Good riddance.

Darkness hovered at the edge of my vision and I knew that I couldn't handle another viewing of so many… I'd go blind.

When I was a kid my momma told me that if I kept reading at night, I'd go blind. Don't think momma ever factored fucking fish people into the mixture.

I got up and turned, ignoring the sounds of happy hooting and cracking bone behind me.

CHAPTER EIGHTEEN

MY LIGHTER DRIED AGAIN RATHER quickly. Didn't realize how cold I had been until the small flickering flame sent a wave of warm comfort shooting down my arm.

Pretty sure my eyes were fucked, or maybe it was my mind. Either way my vision was still blurred. Maybe that was how it was going to be for me: eternity wandering around this labyrinth, slowing losing my marbles.

I'd kill every son of a bitch I found, though.

The light illuminated blurry shapes that I had to squint to make out; I had seen carved tableaus, underground rivers, but no more of the monsters that had destroyed my life. No more noise other than the drifting water, and I crept along in the darkness praying for a way out.

Then I heard the crying and immediately froze in place.

It was all too human, and that was what scared me the most. I placed my hand on an old wooden beam and leaned my head out.

A woman lay against the stone wall, rubbing her face against the cool rock. She was naked and her belly was swollen, massively pregnant.

"Miss him, miss him terribly… can't go home, can't go home…"

I wasn't stupid. I knew a trap when I saw it, I was perfectly prepared to walk right past whatever this was.

"Grady?" I froze in place, my heart stopped, the tension in my chest clenched so tightly I couldn't breathe. "Grady?" She repeated it again.

My dead wife rose shakily to her feet. My last memory of her had been a woman limp and decrepit inside her casket.

Now she was young, her belly swollen with life.

"Renee…" I breathed out, reaching out a trembling hand as she nodded, tears in her eyes. Her skin was warm, and she leaned her head into my palm, tears spiraling down her face as she smiled.

I wrapped her up in my embrace and wept tears of pure joy; reunited, she wasn't dead…

"I missed you so bad."

"I missed you, too."

Didn't want to let go of that embrace. Looking down and kissing the top of her head I whispered, "How are you here?"

My wife shook her head. "I'm not."

She shoved out of my embrace, stepping back, her eyes rolling back into her head, all whites and bloodshot veins.

"Down here in my womb, Grady Pope… never leave, never leave, never leave."

I watched wide0eyed as blood began seeping from between her legs, thick globs running down, coloring her skin so dark it was nearly black.

"*I want the child.*"

Her voice wasn't her own; it was like the deepest point of a suck hole, all rage and crashing water.

She reached down between her legs, cupping her hand and letting the blood congeal inside it before sloshing it in her face and hair.

"*T'usa phalay icha VHI'OCTA!*"

Gibberish words that I didn't understand, but I screamed when the fish came erupting from between her legs in spurt of blood. The placenta dropped behind it with a wet pop, a fully formed bass flopping on the stone floor.

Renee reached down and grabbed it, cuddling and cooing with it like a baby.

I turned and ran into the tunnel, the mocking laughter followed me.

I took tunnels at random. Didn't know where I was going; all I knew was that I was at my wit's and sanity's end. I just wanted to get out, go home, wrap my grandson up and leave this lake behind me.

They'd done it, they'd broken me. I loved Uncertain… I loved the lake…

Knowing what I knew now I swore that if I made it out of this place, I would put the muddy water and the cypress in my rear view mirror.

Images whirled past me: a small cave that contained three pregnant women crouching naked around a flank of meat… a solitary Deep Folk submerged up to its chest in a tidal pool ravishing a naked man with its repulsive hand…

Things that left my eyes bleeding.

There was a blast of humid air and the tunnel disappeared; a wide-open cavern too massive for my puny lighter to illuminate.

I turned around to head back. The entrance was gone, a solid wall of mud and rock all that remained. I pawed at the thick mud desperately, chipping my fingernails and cutting my flesh on the jagged rocks underneath.

Hopelessly, I sank to my knees and let my head thud into the dripping mud wall. There was no way out, and behind me an infinite blackness that probably contained all manner of monstrosities and sights too horrible for me to conceive.

If I just sat here and let myself starve to death, that would bring an end to everything. No more poverty, no more loneliness, just me and the blessed dark.

There was shuffling behind me; no doubt whatever had been down here saw my light and the promise of an easy meal. I flipped over and looked at the dark, ready to scream and cuss at whatever was coming along to end it.

"Grady?"

Sheriff Otis Porter came crawling out the blackness. His clothes were torn, exposing his bare chest and gut that were covered in scrapes and bruises. His face was bone white and haggard looking like he hadn't had a decent meal or sleep in ages.

His legs were both gone, just burned stumps below his knees that kicked back and forth uselessly as he crawled toward me.

I didn't bother moving. Renee hadn't been real, so why should this be real either?

"Grady help me…" He grasped the bottom of my shoes. "For the love of God please!"

I felt the tears water in the back of my eyes; I braced for the end.

"Grady it's so close to your house, the entrance to this place… don't just sit there *dammit!*"

His sudden scream shocked me, and I snapped out of my fugue. "You're not real Otis, you're not here."

Otis groaned and looked down at his legs. "It fucking hurts, Pope. It's hell… the ones who are too old to breed, they eat." His muffled sobs reached me as he looked down at his stumps. "My fucking legs, they ripped them right off and let me crawl away." His eyes twisted wildly in their sockets. "Those warbling laughs, this place, it fucks with your head." Otis twisted a finger on the side of his skull before gripping my leg tight. "*Get up, damn you! Get up!*"

"You aren't here Otis…" I said, flatly refusing to move. My friend looked like I had stabbed him in the heart as he opened wide and bit into my leg, causing me to grunt and clench my teeth in pain.

"I'm here!" He hissed spitting out a bit of my blood. "I've seen how they come and go. That's why they took my legs because God help me, I saw them!"

He twisted like a slug, unable to crawl, and pointed back into the blackness. "It's just there. Just get up and we can swim for it. We can make it!"

My hope was a shriveled thing, like a worm that had been left on a hot sidewalk. The insanity had taken it and left it shivering in a corner, bleeding, begging for a reprieve…

Begging for my wife, my child, and my friends.

Then the other part of me, the part of me that hated, the instinct that had carried me to victory over countless predators over the years, this deep primal part of me appeared…

It kicked the ass of that quivering heap and found its balls.

Still didn't believe that Otis was real but I would be damned if I was going to sit here and die in the dark like a fucking coward.

I clambered to my feet. "Where?" My voice was hoarse; all the screaming had worked the cords over.

Otis pointed a shaking finger. "There's a slope back there, lot of rocks and mud, old houses sunk into the lake, things living in them…" His lip trembled, and I thought he was on the verge of breaking down before he finished. "Big pool of water, like a suck hole. They've been swimming, going in… that's the way out."

Well that was flimsy as shit. Even if it was a way out, there was no way to tell how far it was out of here.

What the hell: I'd rather drown than let myself be eaten by the damn things here.

I stepped over Otis and began walking down the way he came.

"Grady…" He sounded worried; I kept walking.

"Grady!"

I kept walking, ignoring him.

"*Grady, don't leave me here!*"

He wasn't real.

At least that's what I kept telling myself.

The path down the slope had a few jutting rocks that I tried to find steady footholds on. It was hard to see in the gloom. My lighter hadn't been designed to provide light to such big spaces; even now it was sputtering, the butane inside beginning to run dry.

The illusion of Otis was still screaming for me to come back.

That soft part of me that had wanted to curl up and die screamed for me to go back.

Guilt is for those who can't handle survival.

I tested the next rock with my foot and slipped.

Didn't even have time to be surprised before I was tumbling down the hill. I hit a rock, another, something cracked inside of me.

I came to a rest and struggled to breathe, each gasp of air like a knife being dragged through my insides.

Water was close, I could smell it, thought there was a tell-tale splashing too. So close…

I had dropped my lighter when I fell. Now it was just me and the darkness.

Deep Folk were near. I could hear that vile croaking along with footsteps as they sloshed through the mud and water.

Crawled a few feet forward, then a few more, my mind blank, the pain sharp… I touched water, real water, not the mud puddles or shallow pools that were down here.

It was deep, immediately dropping off. The pool went up to my arm and the current tugged at it.

Footfalls behind me…

I threw myself in and let it take me.

The current sucked me down, dragging me along; I held my breath… the pain in my chest made me want to scream.

I don't know how long I twirled through that dark abyss, pulled along like a child's toy swirling towards a drain.

I just knew that I began to float upward.

I saw light.

My lungs felt like they would burst any second, my mind convinced that a hand gripped with talons would circle around my leg and pull me back under.

The sun was shining when I broke the surface, gasping for air.

I tread water ignoring the agony; I was in the river, not the big lake. The trees and terrain here looked familiar but couldn't quite make out where exactly I had found myself.

CATFISH IN THE CRADLE

Something hard hit my back and I yelped, turning in the water, prepared to see some monstrosity looming over me.

Channel Marker 158 jutted from the water, its shadow cast long towards the shore.

CHAPTER NINETEEN

I STUMBLED THROUGH THE TREES, clutching my side. Could have been noon or late morning; the mist had cleared off the lake and now it was just baking heat. The mosquitoes alighted on me as soon as I left the water, smell of blood in the air from a wounded old animal.

Each step was torment. Didn't realize how much I was bleeding. My old bones were done, the adrenaline that had driven me run out.

I was going to get home on sheer determination alone.

Saw Cy's... Luc's old cabin appear out of the trees and thought I heard a booming bark.

My energy disappeared, and darkness took me.

Whispered words, images of a dark cave, old fishing trips, deformed half human fishmen, a god with a bloody face...

I opened my eyes to a haze of blurs and colors I didn't recognize. I was inside a house but my vision was so shitty it could have been an outhouse for all I knew. There was a cool washcloth across my head and I thought I heard muffled voices.

"He's awake."

"How can you tell?"

"Because I can tell. You're so eager to believe every piece of mumbo jumbo I tell you so why can't you just trust my words on anything else?"

I groaned and held up a hand. "You... don't have to talk about me... like I'm not here." Every word took effort and felt like I was eating nails. A familiar hand held mine tight.

"You've got spunk old man; if you came from where Robichaude says you did... you're a hard son of a bitch."

I cracked a small smile. I couldn't help it... hearing Gideon Whyte's voice was music. "What happened to that tight-lipped... respect you heaped on me... the other day?"

Gideon paused and then gripped my hand tighter. "Threw it out with my relationship."

That was the understatement of the year.

"How... how long have I been out?"

Luc's voice came drifting through the haze. "Two days, Mr. Pope. Davis Trucker was by earlier and put some of his old army training to use patching you up. Did what I could with my arts but after all the workings I've been doing over the past few days I'm tapped."

I coughed and something wet gurgled in my throat; a cold washcloth was pressed to my mouth. "Spit it up, there's a good man."

When I finally cleared my mouth I let my head fall down with a weary sigh. "We've got to get the hell out of here."

Both of my friends lapsed into silence.

Something had happened.

"What… happened?" I groaned.

"Apparently your escape from the Cradle didn't go over so well. They've done a world class conjuring and flooded the whole damn river."

"The water hasn't made it up to Shady Glade yet, but Davis said it's close. Tons of debris in the river… nut jobs still out hunting in the middle of the rain." Gideon said, his back against the brightly covered walls.

I tried to sit up and lay back with a groan. my side screaming. Luc laid his hands on me gently.

"Just relax; we're safe for now. The Deep Folk aren't going to be finding this place soon."

We weren't in Luc's cabin; the walls weren't the same… not as much space.

"Where are we?"

"Roads were washed out and the water was coming up quick, took the 175 to Gideon's place."

I groaned. I knew exactly where Gideon Whyte lived.

"Welcome to the *Minute Mother*, Mr. Pope… finest houseboat floating."

We were on the river; any of those crimes against nature could have been swimming under the boat right now.

I felt sick to my stomach.

As if he could tell my pain, I felt a furry snout push itself under my hand. Mojo licked it, and I smiled before I remembered who the dog was supposed to be guarding.

"Lincoln?"

There was a pause from both men; I could blurrily see them look at each other before Luc responded. "Yeah about that…"

A third blurred form joined them. Thought it was a man, judging from how big he was.

A firm hand slipped into mine, I felt the fused skin and immediately knew it was my grandson.

"Grampa, I was worried." His voice was deep. In two days he'd grown into a man.

I wanted to recoil from his touch, but his hand held me firm. "Don't fight Grampa, I've been seeing what's down there too… the mockery of what they once were."

The memory of that gigantic idol dripping mercury flooded through my mind, and a name…

"Don't speak it Grampa. My father's powerful enough to give Mr. Robichaude a tough time repelling."

"Thought your father was run of the mill…" I grunted. My grandson squeezed my hand tighter and I heard Luc gravely respond.

"No, Grady Pope, he's the chieftain."

CATFISH IN THE CRADLE

Took me the better part of a day to recover. According to Luc my body had been through the ringer, something to do with psychic trauma and magical illness that I didn't understand. My eyes slowly came back to me, blurry shapes that had been a struggle to make out gradually giving way to faces when they got close.

Despite his disfigurements, including the ragged lines under his neck that I was disgusted to know were the beginnings of gills, my grandson had grown up to favor me… could have passed as my son judging from the old pictures of me from back in the day.

And he had such things to tell me…

Vhi'octa. The name stuck in my mind but one I didn't dare repeat out loud. Names had power apparently, some magical bullshit that flew right over my head but Luc Robichaude said was important.

Lincoln had grown more powerful. When I wanted to go out on the deck, he carried me like it was nothing. I weighed a good two eighty, two ninety if I had been hitting the bottle hard, and still my grandson carried me as easily as a box.

That new strength had come with new visions in the past two days. His father had reached out to his mind, promising glory and inflicting pain in equal measure.

Luc had interrogated Lincoln mercilessly and now sat on top of the houseboat brooding. Gideon mostly puttered around, usually with a bottle of something in his hand… couldn't blame the kid. He had been deeply in love.

I wanted to find a bottle myself when my grandson explained everything.

Apparently what Luc knew of the Deep Folk added up. They had been driven insane and with every passing generation were growing more and more savage, thanks to the mercury poisoning in their veins. Once peaceful, advanced beings of magic and science reduced to primitive savages worshiping an old statue as a god, seeing the mercury still leaking into the Cradle as holy water.

Lincoln was the first-born without the taint. Pure and strong, he would grow into a powerful chief someday according to Luc if we allowed him down to the Cradle. He'd also lose his mind. There wasn't anything that could stop the madness cooking below us naturally… the Deep Folk would die off eventually. Lincoln's birth to them may have been a sign of salvation, but to Luc it was little more than a genetic quirk due to be snuffed out given time.

All of this was just barely coherent to me, more tall tale than anything. But God help me, I believed it. After all that I had seen and been through, I believed it.

"Why didn't they kill me down there? Or when I fell in the river… woke up and I was alone?"

Lincoln spit into his hand: a bloody tooth. He stared at me with those blank eyes that were becoming more fish like. "Because I'm your grandson. They thought if they kept you there that I would come, follow you down into the dark where my father could then mold me into what he wants."

My grandson chuckled, and I saw the needle teeth haphazardly poking through the flesh of his gums. "Thought they could break your mind down there, but you're a right tough old bastard, Gramps."

I licked my lips, parched to the bone. "If he's this powerful, why can't he come up and get you himself?"

"Because he isn't ready."

Luc Robichaude closed the sliding glass door softly. My grandson eyed the Cajun witch doctor warily as he pulled a seat up to the kitchen counter and began going to work mixing herbs and ingredients, different colored cloths laid out before him.

"He's on the cusp of turning. Soon as those gills of yours come in Lincoln, he'll send his warriors out in force to claim you." The pestle clanked heavily inside the pewter bowl. "And we'll be dead."

Maybe I had spent enough time with Luc Robichaude to know he liked his theatrics, or maybe I was just tired of everything.

"You have a plan to prevent that? Because I'm of the mind we find the nearest speedboat and make it to the nearest high ground. Can't take him if he's five hundred miles away in the middle of the fucking desert."

Luc blew a light covering of bone dust off the cabinet, raising the pewter bowl, concentrating hard. "A good plan, Grady, but your grandson is going to need to spend some time in the water. Don't think there is an overabundance of that in Amarillo."

I practically deflated while Luc set the bowl back down and added a few plants and roots that I couldn't immediately identify.

"When the Deep Folk broke faith with us, we cast enchantments and erected totems in preparation for trying to keep them down there. Carved most of them by hand. A good portion of them have been torn down by the cult, releasing the Deep Folk and other nasties back into the river. But the most important few still stand…"

"Marker 158," I breathed out in realization.

Luc snorted. "Close. We did erect it but it's been vandalized enough times over the years to make it useless. But I think I have a plan for us to find the others. Just need to get back to making these for us." He indicated the half complete mojo bags, turning around and placing a small bone in the red cloth's center, ignoring us as he went about his conjuring.

I knew when a conversation was over. "Need some fresh air."

Lincoln placed a hand on my chest, webbed skin stretching as he firmly held me down. "Grampa, you're not strong enough yet."

I grabbed his arm, trying not to recoil by how moist it was. "Don't tell me what I can and can't do boy. After what I've been through, I want to get out and see the damn river!"

My grandson recoiled as if I had hit him and I hoisted myself up, straining against the pain stitching its way through my belly until I was bent over gasping for breath between my legs.

They had put me on a small couch that was the centerpiece of the boat's living room. Not many folks around here owned houseboats. Lake houses were more peoples speed. Still for some folks the easy floating life was what gave them joy.

CATFISH IN THE CRADLE

The *Minute Mother* was pretty simple as far as most of these boats went; the interior was like a small apartment, brown cupboards and white faux marble countertops. Furniture that must have been a couple of decades old and bought secondhand, a fireplace that had a small television set mounted over it. Must have taken him quite a while to save up for a flat screen. Four wooden chairs around a dinner table that probably came from someone's garage sale, pictures framed on the walls showing various triumphant fishing trips and time spent with Vicky Barnes.

No wonder Gideon had spent most of his time outside for the past day. If Renee had betrayed me I wouldn't have wanted to be surrounded by her smiling face either.

My legs trembled as I stood up and I gritted my teeth. Lincoln slipped a hand under my arm and helped me to my feet as I took a few wobbling steps towards the porch. I reached out and slid the glass door open. My legs were already burning and my head ached, but the fresh air hit me with relief, that muddy pine scent like sweet perfume. The outside of the boat had been painted a bone white that had faded overtime, the paint peeling in places.

We were anchored close to Shady Glade and I had to stop and take in just how much the water had risen since I had come up gasping for air under the channel marker.

It was late afternoon and the sky was dark with rolling thunderheads. There must have been a break in the storm, but I could still smell the rain waiting high overhead. Folks were out in droves here and maybe a hundred yards down at Johnson's Ranch, all of them desperate to get their boats out of the marina before they were crushed against the roof by the rising water.

"I can't go outside Grampa. If someone saw me…"

I stood up straight, reaching out for one of the ladder rungs that led up to the top deck. "Yeah, yeah, I get you. Just leave me to catch my breath for a bit, would you?"

Maybe he knew I couldn't stand looking at that face that was a mockery of a real man's; maybe he thought I just needed some time. Either way he disappeared back into the interior of the houseboat.

Gideon was sitting on a chair, bottle of bourbon halfway empty on the green shag carpet covering the deck. I hobbled over and slowly lowered myself into the chair's matching counterpart. The younger man offered me the bourbon without looking at me.

We drank in silence, Gideon's eyes rooted on the dark cypress forest and letting out a deep sigh as he drank the rest of his glass. That boy who had been happy to see an old man wake up on the table had drifted down the river.

"We were going to get married, you know."

"Never had a fucking clue." I felt bad for the kid. There was no coming back from something like this; hell, I was going to get the fuck out of here when all of this was over.

"Lincoln… kid might be as old as me now."

I nursed the bourbon, letting the warmth run through my veins and didn't respond.

"You're never going to be able to pass him off in society you know."

I grunted.

"Planning to keep him down in the boathouse? Feed him old fish or gator scraps?"

Gideon's tone had become a bitter tirade, one that I cut off as I sat the glass down on the deck's carpet harder than I should have. I leveled a look at the younger man.

"I appreciate your concern Gideon but word to the wise: watch your fucking mouth."

He turned away like I had slapped him. Neither of us said anything else as we nursed our glasses and waited for the sky to fall out.

There was a pounding of heavy footsteps and sloshing water. Davis Trucker was making his way down the pier, cap in hand, fanning his red face as sweat came rolling down. I gave a weary smile as he took a ponderous step onto the houseboat deck, clapping Gideon on the shoulder as he passed.

He put a gentle hand against my shoulder as I started to rise. "Don't get up, old man. Robichaude and Gideon told me what happened." He shook his head in bewildered awe. "Didn't believe any of it until I saw your grandson."

I nodded my head in agreement. "Yeah he's a little bit of a shock, isn't he?"

The thunder boomed overhead, and the rain began again.

"Shit, if the water gets up inside the restaurant again, I'm going to lose it. Repairs cost me an arm and a leg."

I snorted as Davis and Gideon both helped me to my feet and we hobbled into the *Minute Mother's* interior to get out of the rain. "After what I've seen, you might lose an arm and a leg to the things that are in this river."

Davis helped me sit down on the couch before flopping into Gideon's easy chair; the wood creaked in protest as the man forced his massive bulk into the chair while Gideon watched with a pained expression.

"Davis." Luc said simply nodding from the small kitchen. The fat restaurateur nodded back at him.

"Shouldn't you be manning the restaurant, Davis?" Gideon asked quietly, pulling out one of his dining room chairs and sinking into it. He looked smaller than I had ever seen him.

Davis' face darkened, and he gestured for the bottle of bourbon Gideon held lightly in his hand. He tossed it to the big man who caught it with one meaty hand and took a deep swig without bothering to pour any into a glass.

"Man that's some good stuff." He said wistfully as his eyes shifted between the two of us. "Been hard keeping a straight face after what you idiots have told me, especially when Vicky's been asking around if I've seen you, Grady."

Davis snorted. "If she had bothered to show up for work today, I would have told her to just look out the damn window." No one laughed and Davis lapsed back into silence as I asked what had been weighing on my mind.

"Who all do we think is in on this?"

Luc spoke. "Victoria Barnes, Earl Ray and his wife—wouldn't doubt that she's shacked up down in the Cradle. If I didn't need help sewing Gideon up I wouldn't have bothered calling Davis, but my family spoke well of him."

Davis raised the bottle in salute to Luc who tipped his index finger in response.

"What about Scott and Misty Carter?"

Gideon glanced at Luc, who looked confused. "I'm unfamiliar with these people."

"New guy runs the funeral home. Grew up in Atlanta, met him at church… good man."

Davis chuckled. "You *think* he's a good man."

I gestured to the bottle and Davis passed it over. "Only one way to find that out."

"What if he doesn't believe us?" Gideon asked quietly.

Lincoln wandered into the room, each one of his footsteps making a wet plopping sound; Davis blanched a little at the sight of his massively dilated eyes.

"Luckily we have evidence." I pondered darkly.

CHAPTER TWENTY

GIDEON HAD AN OLD HOODIE that barely fit over Lincoln's physique. When my grandson had pulled off the tattered old shirt that had belonged to me in my heyday I recoiled at the sight of his chest. Scales were beginning to push their way out of his skin and the rest of his flesh had begun to take on a sickly brown tone, thought I could hear his bones crunching with every slight movement. A pair of jeans immediately ripped when he pulled them on; his toenails had been replaced with claws.

"I don't think this is going to work very well, Grampa."

"Folks around here mind their own business, son. Just act normal and no one will notice."

Davis had a hand against one of the ladder rungs, keeping himself steady. "Unless they get a good look at his face, that is."

I fixed him with a death glare as Luc appeared, passing out small red pouches to each of us. "Hopefully we won't be needing this, but if something nasty comes our way, recite the Lord's prayer a few times and that should do the trick."

Davis pulled at the string. "What's in this?"

Luc grabbed his hand. "It's a conjure sack, bit of magic in a bag, and if you unwind that string my enchantments will unravel with it."

The restaurateur coughed then shrugged and placed the bag in his pocket. "Whatever you say, Robichaude. Heard the rumors but I never believed any of that hoodoo crap."

Luc wrapped a necklace of bone, alligator teeth, and other little charms around his neck. "Best start believing, Mr. Trucker."

The wind howled and rain swept the pier as we left, Gideon locking the *Minute Mother's* doors behind us.

The water was starting to come up fast now, the swell upriver probably feeding into the current faster. People were beginning to get desperate with lines of trailers waiting at the ramp to pull their boats out of the water. There were blaring horns and angry fists as folks were soaked senseless under the never-ending downpour. We walked past them, hopefully projecting that people should mind their own business. Lincoln's shoulders were stooped, his head bowed as we made our way down the pier.

No one paid us mind, much to my relief. I hadn't fully recovered yet and Lincoln had to support me when we reached the cinderblock steps leading up to the muddy parking lot in front of Shady Glade. We decided on taking two trucks: Gideon would drive Lincoln and I in his truck while Davis would take Luc in his.

Lincoln eased me into the back seat of the extended cab truck; Gideon slid into the driver's seat and cranked on the heat. My grandson climbed up next to me and shut the door a little harder than he probably intended, then we were off.

It was about a ten-minute drive from Shady Glade to Scott's house next to the old ammunition plant in Karnack; Gideon turned on music, a local rock station out of Shreveport and lapsed into his own little world.

Lincoln was quiet too, though I occasionally caught him giving me furtive glances before turning away quickly when I noticed. Hadn't spent this much time with him since he was little.

Since he was little... God, five days ago seemed like a lifetime, hell...

"Grampa..." I glanced over at him, still seeing the human features despite the grotesquely huge pupils and mixed teeth. "What was my mom like?"

The question caught me off guard; I hadn't really expected him to be curious about his mother... didn't think something like him would even care.

"She was... she was... beautiful, smart, and much smarter than your grandmother or me."

I laughed and told Lincoln a story of when his mother was eight and had to dress up as a state for a school pageant; Renee had been busy pulling a double shift down at the diner in Jefferson, leaving me to help my daughter. Using my skills I had made the shittiest rendition of Florida that ever existed, old cardboard and torn mattress scrawled with Florida facts and doodles. As parental projects went it was a pretty crappy effort, but it was the best that I was able to make. She had inevitably lost for best costume, the other students and parents looking at the poor girl with mixtures of pity and anger.

Sammie Jo had taken those looks with pride, taking pleasure with the costume her Dad had put effort and time into, even if it had come out looking like a half-aborted alligator.

Told her I would give her a twenty if she kept it from her mother too.

When I was finished, Lincoln was smiling; disconcerting with all of those pointed teeth.

"What about you, son? Robichaude didn't really explain much about…" I gestured to him. "This."

Lincoln lifted his hand and stared at the webbed veins that now had an odd green tinge to them, patterns forming on the skin. "I don't really know Grampa. when Vicky watched me that second day, she made me drink the mercury… part of their god… my father, he's been whispering in my head ever since."

I pondered on this for a moment, feeling kinship that I had tried to force for the past few days on bond of blood alone. He was a good kid, couldn't help what he was.

"Is he whispering to you now?"

Lincoln nodded and his eyes dilated, becoming a few sizes smaller. "He wants me to kill you and come down to him, down where you escaped from."

I suddenly felt nauseous and it had nothing to do with the bumpy car ride.

"I don't want to do that, Grampa. I don't want to be this way." His fists, talons and all, closed and I saw pinpricks of tears in his eyes. "There's no fighting it. Couple of hours I won't be able to stand the air... I'll have to go down."

My grandson's voice never wavered, despite how afraid I could tell he was, and it let me know right then and there that despite his appearance and lineage, a part of him was still a man and kin. I was going to help him even if it spurred that heart attack that killed me. Just this once blood was thicker than water.

"We're here."

Gideon's gruff voice interrupted any further conversation as we trundled slowly up the path towards Scott's house. The funeral home director's car was parked in the driveway, and I thought I could make out the flashing screen of a TV through the living room window. Davis and Luc pulled in behind us as Gideon killed the engine and got out of the truck.

The rain was coming down hard as we made our way up the steps and out of the grey torrent behind us. Lincoln and Luc were both immediately on edge.

"Something isn't right." The Cajun hoodoo man stepped up and placed his hand against the door and recoiled with a curled lip. "Yeah, bad juju."

None of us had thought to bring guns other than Gideon's pistol, a .22 revolver that he clutched for dear life.

Lincoln stepped forward. "Let me go first."

I thought of the hole that led down to the river in Scott's basement. If some fish faced monster had come up…

"Knock the door down, boy."

Lincoln didn't have to be asked twice as he kicked the door. The hinges groaned in protest. He kicked it again and the door came free of the frame in a splintering crash of wood.

The inside of the house was covered in shadows. Faint voices echoed from the living room.

Gideon stepped up next to Lincoln, pistol clenched in his hand. Shivers ran up and down his arm and the barrel of the gun wavered from side to side as he scanned the hallway.

"Davis, watch the cars. Make sure that nothing comes sneaking up behind us. Lincoln stay with him." My grandson hesitated but backed down when he saw the look on my face.

I motioned to Gideon and Luc. We dove into the house, taking a right and heading into the living room.

The television was on, an old rerun of *The Andy Griffith Show* playing on the set.

A corpse sat on the couch. A black woman, the wispy grey hairs struggling to hold their places on the top of her wrinkled head. They'd done her up good, the people who followed those damn things that lived under the lake. Fish were painted across her, bright yellow and greens contrasting with her dark skin. Catfish, gar, bass, bream, they'd taken their time to craft each one unique.

Her mouth was open, and her tongue and eyes had been removed. I almost vomited when I saw the worms squirming around inside the empty sockets.

"Oh my God," Gideon whispered as he saw the shining hooks that had pierced her lips, corks and leads hanging from the metal like some sort of perverse Christmas trees. Algae had been splattered over her along with a crown of grey cypress moss.

"An offering to Vhi'octa. The abomination will accept the dead flesh so it can nest its putrid deformed offspring." Luc spat the name and the purpose of the corpse with disgust. "We need to find Scott."

I grunted and pointed at the basement door hanging ajar. Luc and Gideon didn't have to be told to keep their voices down.

The stairs were dark and at the bottom I thought I could hear water splashing. My heart pounded in my chest as I took the first creaking step, flicking the light switch in vain. I heard a click and the steps became illuminated by Gideon's flashlight.

The bottom of the landing was a formless mass of black water. Taking ginger steps that barely masked our footfalls we descended until the water was lapping at the edges of my boots. I took a deep breath that did nothing to calm my nerves and took that first trembling step. The water was warm, and I nearly choked on my own bile as it came rumbling up my throat. Choking it down, I tested the waters until I found the floor of the mortuary.

The water was up to my waist. Knick knacks and other pieces of detritus floating through the grimy water.

"Scott!" I hissed, my voice echoed off the walls and drifted back with the light lapping of water against the linoleum tiles.

Gideon was beginning to pant behind me and I was sure that his heartbeat matched my own that was pounding away like a jackhammer. His flashlight swerved through the darkness left and right, bouncing off the walls and shining towards every little sound.

"Calm yourself!" Luc hissed from the rear.

There was deep croak from somewhere deeper in the basement.

My hand leapt to my throat and the mojo bag dangling from around it.

"Grab that magic tight, Grady Pope, and say your prayers," Luc warned behind me.

I told myself that when this was all over, I was going to box that boy behind the ears for playing creepy hoodoo man.

Never had spent much time down here when we had Saturday night poker. Don't think Scott had ever let anyone down here. Dignity for the dead or not, I didn't particularly want to go tramping around where corpse upon corpse was stored in freezers. Uncertain didn't have a high death rate but it did happen, and the thought that someone I might have had coffee with once upon time was floating underneath the water, hollowed out, ready to bump into me…

It sent chills running up my spine.

The darkness opened up to reveal a corridor that branched off in opposite directions. The water was beginning to eat at the wallpaper with damp lines mildewing the material, dark wet wood showing beneath it.

There was a splashing sound from the right, louder than the lapping water, and what sounded like a grunt.

"We're going left, yeah?"

I scowled behind me at Gideon, pretending that I wasn't scared shitless. "Don't let your balls shrivel up now. Water's not even cold."

Gideon gritted his teeth as Luc waded up and put his hand on the moldering wall, staring down the dark hallway. "If you don't want to go first Gideon, I will, but I would like that pistol of yours. unlike Mr. Pope, I'm not comfortable with a twitchy trigger finger behind me."

Gideon looked ashamed of himself and wiped the beads of sweat from his forehead, clicking the safety on and steadying himself against the wall. For the first time I noticed how old he seemed now, his experiences the past few days no doubt aging him fast.

"No, I'm good. Just need to get ahold of myself. Been awhile since I've been this scared."

Luc pressed a hand against Gideon's chest. "Our Father. who art in heaven…"

I listened to him recite the entire prayer and when he was finished Gideon stood a little straighter, his hand no longer trembled. "Bit of belief goes a long way."

Didn't bother asking; just trusted that the mumbo jumbo did its thing.

"I'll take point, Mr. Pope."

I wanted to chuckle, but even talking with lowered voices was too much for my liking.

Gideon sloshed past me through the water, handing his flashlight to me while he aimed the pistol down the narrow blackness.

Wasn't more than thirty feet to the end of the hall and we rounded the corner into another hall. It had two doorways that we could see; the flashlight couldn't pierce the stretching dark that remained. One of the doors had been ripped from its hinges; it was floating on the water close to us, giant gashes torn down the aged wood.

There was a sputtering light from inside the door.

The three of us glanced at each other before I clicked off, the flashlight drowning us in a womb of blackness. The light fizzed, electricity vainly trying to keep the fluorescent contraption lit. There was a grunting followed by a pleased croak.

We inched forward, each step on the submerged floor careful not to disturb the water lest whatever horror inside hear us and attempt to sate its inhuman desires. I put a hand on Gideon's shoulder and I felt Luc's hand on mine. We clustered around the door's entrance, straining to see within.

It was the freezer room where Scott stored the bodies until burial or cremation. There were about ten units and four of them had been ransacked, the iron drawers torn out in huge metallic gashes. Four corpses floated in the water, naked, in various positions.

Two Deep Folk stood in the water; Scott and Misty Carter were strapped down to two gurneys by thick strands of moss. Scott's mouth was bloody; small crawdads feasted heavily on the spluttering gurgles of blood that bubbled in his mouth. Misty was screaming, a dull sound that came out as a muted grunting; her mouth had been sewn shut.

CATFISH IN THE CRADLE

Victoria Barnes stood between them, a bathing suit top showing off her ample cleavage. She was clutching a brown cup that looked like it had been carved from a piece of driftwood. Her eyes had a mad gleam that transformed into a look of ecstasy as one of the Deep Folk grabbed her arm and warbled something in its guttural tongue.

"Soon, soon, sweetie. I know our lord needs more."

My eyes twitched and I felt that heavy blanket fall over my mind, but the sight of the monstrosities didn't feel nearly close enough now to break my mind. Probably Robichaude's juju at work.

Gideon was biting his lip hard enough to draw blood now. His breath had hitched in his chest and he stared in undisguised hate and hurt at the woman who until a few days ago had been the love of his life.

The insane waitress reached under the water, searching for the creature's loins. It threw back its head in a warbling hiss, its eyes blinking as its jaws clacked.

The other Deep Folk sloshed forward and shoved its compatriot away, seizing Vicky's arm in a vice grip and dragging it under the water to its own disgusting organ.

"Boys, boys, there's plenty for you both but we best get this done, yes?" Vicky said it all with a smile, pushing off the creature with a laugh as she precariously balanced the cup in her hand. The Deep Folk both backed off to the edge of the room and bowed their heads as Vicky raised the cup above her head.

"Blessed be he who was formed from ancient blood, from innumerable worlds and times. Let him who comes at the tide speak what he wishes to us now."

Vicky lifted the cup onto Scott's lips and poured the concoction into his mouth. He struggled momentarily, his lips attempting to spit out whatever it was that the insane woman was pouring in his mouth.

Then his struggling ceased.

Misty began screaming from behind her lips and struggling heavily until one of the Deep Folk stepped forward and pressed a hand down into her chest hard enough to cause her eyes to bulge. She began breathing heavily, trying to regain her wind.

There was a hissing sound and I saw what looked like white melted candle wax slide off of Scott's face as his ragged breathing became shallow and then stopped, replaced by what sounded like boiling water.

Knew he was dead. Poison probably, but who knows what Vicky slid down his throat.

There was a heavy weight on the air and then a gust of wind like a car had rushed past me. Scott Carter sat up on the table.

I bit my tongue to keep from gasping; his eyes were gone, replaced by liquid mercury that ran in twin waterfalls down his cheek and into the water.

"Vi'hocta, Mighty Warrior, Purity of Blood, we welcome you up from the Cradle and ask for your guidance." Vicky parroted the words like a true believer; her back was to us and her head bowed.

The two Deep Folk fell to their knees the water coming up to their waists as Scott opened his mouth, another torrent of mercury running down his chin and into the water.

"*Ch'aot...*" The words came bubbling from Scott's mouth, but his lips didn't move. "*F'jos a'eko sama.*"

The language was foul and guttural. I looked at Luc to make sure my eyes weren't lying, that they'd worked some kind of mojo on our friend. A grim nod of his head confirmed it.

The voice reminded me of mighty beasts ruling a world long forgotten. Of times and places so unfathomable in their horror that a man like me and as tough as I was wouldn't have lasted a night against the things that had populated that place. This was the voice of the Deep Folk's chieftain, and it was a monument to things better left unseen under the sun.

Vicky nervously fidgeted before hesitantly replying. "We can't find the last of the infernal channel markers, Master. the Robichaudes hid them too well. Your insight... your guidance... we pray for it."

The thing inside Scott reached out with a stiff hand, the movement making a sloshing sound; the bottom of his arm was dark and discolored. It backhanded Vicky with contemptuous ease, sending her sprawling into the water.

A splattering of mercury hit the water as the woman pulled herself up, tears shining bright in her eyes.

"*CASHAX VOM BHOTCA LOSH!*"

Luc stepped forward before I could stop him. "If they bothered to think instead of fucking beasts then you'd already be drowning the world."

Scott's sightless eyes looked up. His hair had liquefied, the metal running down his face like a blasphemous baptism.

"Robichaude" The word came tumbling out like a curse as the Deep Folk growled and flanked the corpse sitting on the table. Gideon and I mimicking the motion with Luc.

"My Lord, this was your sacrifice of flesh before the magician and this limp dick old—"

Gideon pulled the trigger on the gun and Vicky's head snapped back. Her eyes didn't even have time to register shock before she toppled forward.

The two Deep Folk roared and surged forward. Luc raised his hand quickly and blew a spray of yellow powder into both of the creature's revolting faces. Both monsters stopped in their tracks, one of them mere inches from Gideon's head. Their eyes bulged, and they grasped at their throats, their gills undulated, bodies relaxing.

"*Hajah ucolan* Robichaude.*"

Scott's mouth was still open; his bare chest had begun to dissolve into more of the liquid metal… wouldn't be much left of him at this rate.

"Gideon, Mr. Pope, get Mrs. Carter out."

I didn't question the order, sloshing through the water within a hand's breadth of the two Deep Folk, staring slack jawed at nothing.

Scott turned its head towards me, nose dissolving. The throat clucked and made warbling croaking noises, the sightless eyes fixing me with a look of intense hatred.

"Fuck you," I replied as firmly as I could, my insides a storm of nausea as half of his face dissolved down to the bone.

More words in their foul language of murky water and forgotten things, most of them directed at me but were spat in Luc's direction.

CATFISH IN THE CRADLE

I tore the restraints loose. Misty sat up immediately and stared wide eyed at Scott who ignored her, his stomach dissolved the sputtering light strobing through his chest.

The thing that possessed him continued speaking, its inhuman will driving it forward. The warbling tongue of the monster somewhere deep in the Cradle never ceased its unpronounceable and foul curses.

"That's enough of that." Luc said calmly as he stepped up to Scott's corpse and drove an iron nail through its forehead.

The flesh parted easily, eyelids shutting to cover the empty sockets before my friend's whole body liquefied into mercury, running off the examination table and into the water.

Luc looked weary as he balanced himself against the examination table. Misty was sobbing behind her stitched lips.

"Lord in your mercy. may the gates open for him. Pardon his transgression, give him eternal rest, and spare him from the fire." The Cajun hoodoo man crossed himself before turning to face the two Deep Folk.

"Go back to the Cradle. tell your chieftain I've come, that he is mistaken to think that he will triumph here, that there is still time to bargain."

The Deep Folk nodded, their eyes dull as they backed away, the shadows closing in around them. The water got deeper and both monstrosities sank away, slipping under the surface without so much as a ripple.

"You're going to have to teach me some of that." Gideon replied in awe, slipping a hand around Misty to support her.

Luc waved a hand. Despite the damn chill in the air I could make out beads of sweat trickling down his forehead. "It… isn't as easy as… it looks." He was panting and leaning heavily against the table, his eyes drooping. "Once the spell's done… really takes…" I caught him before he could slip under the water and supported him under my shoulders.

"Let's get the fuck out of here."

Gideon didn't have to be told twice and the two of us, supporting Luc and Misty, waded towards the door.

There was a splashing sound behind us.

I immediately whirled around. Nothing. But after the past few days I had learned it was never just nothing.

"Gideon…"

The younger man's eyes began darting around the room as we began to back up, Vicky's corpse floating on the water and the three corpses floating close to their freezer units.

Three corpses…

There had been four earlier.

The corpse of an old white man disappeared under water, a woman who had been mangled in a car accident, another old man succumbed to a heart attack… like twisted ropes had wrapped around them and dragged them into a cold embrace.

Vicky's corpse followed suit.

Gideon turned and immediately began sprinting as fast as he could, helping Misty.

A hand gripped my leg underneath the water, pulling backward and sending me toppling face first into the grimy muck. I twirled around and struggled to breathe, releasing

CATFISH IN THE CRADLE

Luc and kicking downward with my free foot. My boot kicked right through the bone; felt like kicking a damn brick wall.

Broke the surface gasping, my old lungs begging me for relief.

One of the deformed half-breeds stood over me, blind like the one I had saw in the cradle, blue worms latched onto its eyes. Its hands darted to my throat quick as a snake, nails digging into my throat.

Couldn't breathe, red appeared at the edge of my vision. I dragged a hand across its face the skin feeling like rough sandpaper.

I was nearly gone. More of them rose from the water, their tongues clicking a warbling battle cry as they crowed in around me. Loathsome words I didn't understand bubbled out of the leader's throat as it opened its mouth wide, its head flopping grotesquely, teeth elongated to swallow my head whole.

Two more crowded close and began to vomit hot mercury into my face. I didn't even have time to sputter as the last of my strength left me and I accepted the end.

Suddenly there was air. I gasped as the inbred abomination went flying, hissing in pain as it landed against the wall. My throat was sore, felt swollen... hurt to even breathe.

Lincoln stood panting, his arms outstretched, glancing at the other four Deep Folk around him.

"USHTA FALAY VHI'OCTAX."

Lincoln's eyes blinked once, his teeth biting into the flesh of his lips, the small nub of his tongue lolling behind them.

"Submit to me."

The Deep Folk of the closest to me stepped forward nodding, the top of its forehead scraping against the low hanging ceiling as it lowered its head in supplication. Lincoln shrank back as the dripping hands made signs in the air and reached for him.

"Savant told me what I had to do, told me that it was for the good of the family… but I don't think that's true."

The Deep Folk faltered in the water. their eyes not daring to meet Lincoln's.

"Go back, back down… now…"

The lead one immediately shrank into the water, barely a ripple marring the surface as it disappeared. The rest of the fishmen followed suit, my grandson's will absolute.

Lincoln didn't say a word as he reached down and picked me up "Come on, Grampa."

He picked Luc up, mercifully unconscious and floating face up, then carried both of us as easy as babes up the flight of stairs and out of the house of death.

CHAPTER TWENTY-ONE

DAVIS BREWED SOME HOT TEA in the kitchen as most of us sat around one of the check print tables. We'd returned to Shady Glade and Davis had roared in and ordered everyone out; something about flood control. What townsfolk were there vacated in a hurry, none of them eager to be on the other side of the massive restaurateur's boot.

My throat felt like someone had shoved a red-hot poker down it. Every breath burned and stroked another fit of coughing.

Davis and Gideon had snipped the stitches keeping Misty's mouth shut. She had sequestered herself in the far corner of the restaurant, quiet mourning every once in a while giving way to uncontrollable sobs. Didn't blame her; would have joined myself if the wracking sobs didn't make me feel like I was swallowing glass.

Luc was sprawled out on a table, sleeping like the dead. Lincoln had dropped him with little fanfare onto the table before stalking off to the nearest window and staring out at the sweeping rain. Took a chair next to him. Gideon was sitting not far away, lost in his own misery sipping on a soda that Davis had plopped in front of him. The big man forbade alcohol inside his establishment.

Alcohol, my pipe, hell even some chewing tobacco despite my long years without it, I was without my comforts or distractions for the first time since Sammie Jo had reappeared under my dock.

Conversation in the truck aside, might have been time to actually talk to the boy.

"Thinking hard?" I grunted. Those black bulbs inside his head blinked, the hoodie that Gideon had given him torn in a few places.

"Thinking about what my father said... about what he wants." His voice was beginning to take on that peculiar croaking halt, the words coming harder for him.

"You aren't your daddy's slave, Lincoln. Only person who can decide that is you."

Lincoln's eyes never left the pouring rain. Didn't know if my words had any kind of impact on him. Always had been shit at trying to comfort people.

"The water looks cool... I want it so bad." He let out a long hissing sigh. "It won't be long... now, feel the pressure, my heads hurting real bad now. Feel less like you, not weak, not meaty... not real... I can see cities and things so ancient... I don't want to go down there."

CATFISH IN THE CRADLE

There were no tears. Good boy knew better than to show weakness, but it damn well struck a chord with me. Kid had been thrust into the world, aged up overnight, actively hated by me at times, and still he was clinging to what he saw in us.

Not much I could do about that, but hell, I was the only decent kin the kid had left. At least the only one who might actually give a damn about him. Might have been something there I could relate to.

"Come on boy…" I said patting my grandson's arm; he looked up, confused.

"Where are we going?"

I gave a weary grin and turned away as Davis walked out with the tea. "There are a few things a man needs to experience before life begins stealing your joy."

Davis sat the tea down. "Get a hankering to take a walk?"

"Just to Gideon's houseboat. Won't be too farther. Lincoln and I need a little family time. Besides I don't reckon we will be planning our next move until Robichaude wakes up."

The Cajun hoodoo man still slept like the dead, his mouth lightly hanging open.

Davis chuckled darkly. "Fair point. Might want to bring his dog in; don't know if we are going to have to find higher ground lickety-split."

I nodded and headed out the door, grabbing an old Crip's Camp cap and putting it on my head, hunching in my jacket as the cold whipping rain splashed my face. Lincoln lumbered after me, his hoodie down, his mixed pale and muddy brown flesh soaking up the water as it hit.

Took a bit to watch him lift his hands, lips stretching into a smile that put me off. It wasn't a human smile; couldn't put my fingers on why it was wrong. Guess I had just never seen a real man look at water like a god.

"Come on boy," I said it as gently as I could. My grandson was a good foot and a half taller than me now and if what he thought was true was beginning to happen… Well, I would just rather not be on the bad side of an inhuman killing machine without my local witch doctor to back me up.

Walking as fast as I could we made our way down to the pier. Wasn't too much longer before the whole thing would be underwater. All the boats were gone now except for Gideon's houseboat; that would stay anchored until the water went back down.

Though if what Luc said was true maybe it would just rain until the whole world drowned.

The water was coming through the planks on the pier as we passed the empty slips and eased up the ramp onto the shag carpet deck. I was virtually out of breath already, throat was burning away and after a couple of days of exertion I was feeling my damned age. Wrinkling up like a prune… even with whatever juju Luc worked on me.

Slid open the glass door. Mojo lifted his head off the deck; the big white dog stared at the two of us with disinterest before laying his head back on the floor with a weary chuff. Scratched his ears as I passed "Good boy." The dog's tail wagged.

"Sit down wherever," I told my grandson as I dug into Gideon's liquor cabinet. The boy had good taste; I might have been a bourbon man but damn me to hell if I was going to turn down a scotch when it was in my face.

Two glasses, an unopened bottle (I'd apologize later), and I returned to my grandson who was sitting awkwardly at the dinner table, his head twitching as he looked at the splashing rain on the river surface.

Tapped the glass in front of him. "How much will you have?"

He looked nervous, those black pupils squinted double eyelids blinking "I... I don't know, Grampa."

"Better make it a double."

The golden-brown comfort poured easily out of the bottle, and when it was nearly a quarter of the way full I paused and poured my own glass, gently sliding the first one over to Lincoln.

Lowered myself carefully. My back was sore and beginning to ache. Sweet relief flooded through me as I leaned back.

"What is this, Grampa?"

"Man should at least have a drink once in his life."

Lincoln went to drink. "No, no, son, don't just start unless you're alone." I raised my own glass. "You toast when you're in good company."

He mimicked my motion and I searched for some kind of joy to toast to in the darkness of the past few days.

Only one came to mind really.

"To family." I said.

"To... family," Lincoln croaked in reply.

I clinked his glass and downed the warm liquid. It went down smoother than the engine grease I usually funneled down; didn't even flinch when it burned my throat something fierce.

Lincoln looked almost giddy as he tossed the glass back; draining it quickly and then immediately began coughing. Smiling behind my glass, I watched my grandson stumble over to the sink and fumble with the knobs, eagerly lapping up the water that came streaming, letting it fall across the back of his neck and onto the wrinkled skin.

Was thinking about pouring me another when I saw that wrinkled skin split open around his neck, gills that eagerly moved back and forth to breathe in the water.

I gripped my glass tight, probably busting all sorts of blood vessels in my hands, couldn't help that though all I could do was watch. Watch as another piece of humanity flaked off my grandson like fall leaves.

He stood back up with a grunting sigh and lumbered back towards me. "That… didn't taste… good."

I licked my lips and tried to smile. "Yeah it ain't supposed to. A lot of people have met their end drinking."

Poured myself another glass. My head was hurting. Probably needed water but looking at my grandson decided I'd rather drink another double to forget.

"Fine American tradition, drinking. Back before either of our times, they used to run boatloads of booze from stills up to Mooringsport…" I sipped, trying to ignore the quivering gills and letting the sauce drift my imagination off to better times.

"Yeah, Grampa, few of those boats went missing, you know."

Glad to hear he wasn't croaking anymore. Talking might have been doing some good... as if I knew how to deal with something like this.

"How did you know that boats went missing back in the old days?"

Lincoln lifted his hand. The webbing looked strange, more animal; he pointed a finger at the side of his head. "I can see it in my head like I was there. My cousins coming up out of the Cradle to snatch... shiners... didn't care about the alcohol... only the meat."

The croaking was back. I felt my mouth go dry and I hastily swallowed a little bit more. "Your father squawking at you?"

Lincoln shook his head. "No just something... we can all do."

We. Didn't like that...

Whatever else may have happened, it was interrupted when Mojo lifted his head and immediately let out a deep, booming bark.

Jumped in my seat. Never knew a dog could make a noise that deep... had mostly mutts growing up and never any as big as Mojo.

"What is it, boy?"

Mojo barked again and made his way over to the door, pawing at the glass.

I stood up; ambling over and sliding open the door, the giant ball of white fur went barreling out the door almost bowling me over... I cursed to high heaven as I saw the giant ball of white disappear down the pier.

"Dammit." I muttered, waving my hat back and forth. Lincoln had risen from his seat, those giant eyes not looking concerned or bothered in the slightest. "Need to see to that… sorry it cut the time a little short."

Lincoln shook his head and gave his best smile, creeping me the hell out. "You go do what you have to do, Grampa. I think I'm going to stay out here awhile."

My heart tightened in my chest. "You sure?"

"I'll be fine; rain just feels good is all."

It was then and there I decided that I needed to wake Luc up, and if stirring him regular wouldn't work then I was going to have to ask Davis if he would break out his smelling salts from his old boxing days.

Lincoln trod out onto the soaking green shag carpet and lifted his face towards the sky, the flesh on his cheeks a dull olive color.

I felt like I was about to be sick. I followed in the mutt's escape path down the pier.

The water was over the boards now. The planks were just under the surface, still took it slow didn't want to slip and fall into the murky river. It was beginning to lap at the bottom of the stone steps before I got to them. Had to tell Davis we might want to pull up tacks; water was coming up quick now.

Gideon was waiting at the door, holding it open and gesturing me inside. Davis had the heaters going full blast now; grateful for that considering the chill bumps running up my arm. I was drenched, and my legs were on fire from running. Vision was a little blurry too, and I wondered if they had bothered to put the reading glasses that Renee had made me get years back on the houseboat.

Luc was sitting up on the edge of the table, one arm resting on his knee, hand holding his forehead. The other drooped to his side and scratched Mojo's massive head.

"I tell you, feel like I went ten rounds at Johnson's Landing."

Davis slipped a cup of hot tea into Luc's hand; he took it gratefully and began sipping on it slowly.

Misty still sat shell shocked over in the corner. Didn't know if she was going to recover… hell, after the whammy my mind had undergone seeing the Deep Folk, I didn't blame her a bit.

"Where's Lincoln?" Luc rasped out, glancing around the restaurant to make sure that he hadn't missed him hiding in some corner of the diner.

"He's out on the houseboat deck, taking in the rain."

Luc snorted and sipped more of tea. "That doesn't sound comforting." The hoodoo man read my mind exactly.

Gideon asked the questions on everyone's mind. "Anybody else hear…" He took a gulping breath; couldn't say Vicky's name, not yet. "That they're looking for the channel markers?"

Luc nodded. "Not many of them left either. Government removed a few… kids out looking for scares, messed up the etchings on a few others. Marker 158 out by your place, Mr. Pope, was the last one my Pop made, trying to seal the entrance to the Cradle." He downed the tea with a bitter gasp. "Wish that one wasn't so well known."

That was a sentiment I shared; I had run off kids often enough from it. Reckoned more than a fair share would have made it through.

"So how many are left?" Davis asked, reaching out to refill his cup. Luc shrugged. "Don't know. My grandfather Stefan used to keep a map of them at the old house. I don't expect that's still intact."

The image of that burned-out wreck floated through my mind, bodies hanging still in the humidity.

Yeah, didn't expect that map to be dandy.

"Best I've got are a few drawings and etchings that my sister made when Pop would take us out to check on them. I was barely walking at the time, so couldn't much say where they were, but I know it was remote enough that the chances they've been ruined are slim."

Davis patted the young man on his back. "You have them on you?"

Luc shook his head. "Out in the houseboat. Bastienne knew her way around a pencil. The drawings are pretty."

Maybe for the first time I realized that the younger man was alone in the world. I mean, I'm sure he had some kinfolk, but no direct family, no one that was going to be waiting for him to come home.

Odd kinship we had on that front. Only difference was that he could still meet a nice girl, drop a couple of brats, and lead a happy life. My wife was rotting in the ground and my grandson was turning into a fish. Didn't think there was much hope left for me to be raising any kind of family.

"Gideon and I will go and get them; you're still recovering."

CATFISH IN THE CRADLE

Luc looked like he was about to protest, but one withering look from me and he sat back down. Mojo man or not, he wasn't going to go against me.

I shrugged at Gideon and he fell into line easily.

The rain was pouring down hard now, like the world knew we were onto shutting down these fish-faced fuckers for the last time.

"Have to hurry or else we are going to be swimming out to your place."

Gideon nodded, shivering hard under the scathing rain; it was coming down like razorblades now.

Water had come up again in the few minutes that I had been inside, and I grumbled to myself that I had just barely gotten warm before I was back out here in it. My ankles were drenched; could barely feel the wooden planks beneath as I waded forward as slow as I could. Gideon was right behind me and didn't look like he was in the mood to be rushing either. Both of us were well aware of what could be creeping up under the waves.

About halfway down I noticed that Lincoln was standing on the deck. He cut an imposing figure in the grey streak-stained sky, dark and towering, every bit a man of strength.

Ten feet tall, a crowd of Deep Folk had surfaced next to the houseboat. None of the half-baked inbred monsters; a congregation of primordial terror. Their heads were bowed to Lincoln, who scratched wildly at his arms. Every scratch peeled off more of his skin revealing the dull browns and greens of the scales that had been forming under the surface.

My heart jumped in my chest and I leapt forward. Never even saw the half-breeds that were lurking under the water until they rose silently on the dock in front of us.

Gideon froze and grasped for his gun that he didn't have.

The mismatched fishmen lurched towards us only to a freeze to rumbling, "*Wait!*"

Lincoln was reaching toward us with a single hand. The syndactyly had transformed into a thick membrane connecting his fingers, and bony brown scales ran up his arm like an infection. His face was the only thing close to the same, that last little bit of human. Spines had ripped through is clothing that now hung in a fucked up mockery rather than to cover anything.

From the water, one of the half-breeds hauled itself up onto the deck, its skin a dark black and olive green, pasty black hair sticking to its face.

"Never was going to hurt you… Lincoln… but he can't hold you back…anymore—" Savant Huber smiled wickedly, a long tongue running across his putrid lips, "You're… coming home… with me now…"

"*Like hell!*" I shouted. The half-breeds growled at me, but a swift roar from the mercury-stained wretch halted them.

Lincoln stared at his cousin and then at the two of us.

"Don't kill them… and I'll go with you willingly…"

"Done." Savant Huber, or whatever its real name was, sounded almost giddy.

There was a silent pressure that passed over the lake, like the shockwave of an explosion. The half-breeds vanished into the water. the Deep Folk stepped backward into the deepening water, disappearing into the rain. Savant fell backward, letting the river claim him.

All of them gone until Lincoln was alone on the deck. He looked pained raising one of his hands.

I knew a goodbye when I saw it.

He stepped off into the water, the river closing around him like a long-lost child.

Didn't cry, didn't shout. A good Pope boy until the last.

CHAPTER TWENTY-TWO

WE FOUND LUC'S SPELL BOOK easily enough, resting next to his clutter of mumbo jumbo.

We had walked in fear the rest of the way down the pier. Can't blame us for that; I didn't exactly reckon that the bastard would actually keep his word. Maybe he was worried that Lincoln would come shooting back up to rejoin us if he actually drug us down deep.

The water had come up to our chests and we were practically swimming, holding the book wrapped up in an old hoodie that Gideon pulled out of a closet.

Luc was standing on the shore, his eyes dark, scanning the water. "Saw them go at the end."

I shoved the book into his arms and stalked past him, unwilling to tell him that wading through the water had taken a lot out of me. Unwilling to let anyone see me squeezing back the tears as my face contorted in rage and sorrow.

I found a nice corner of the diner to curl up in, around the corner closest to the back wall. Let myself go then, tears fell down.

The rest knew better than to come asking.

Composed myself after a couple of minutes, didn't take long for the rage to overcome the sorrow, and when I walked back around the corner no one cared to comment, something I was grateful for.

Davis was whispering to Misty who was resting her head in her hands. She had come out of her silence and occasionally sipped her tea between the tears.

Didn't blame her.

Luc and Gideon had spread three old pieces of sketch paper across the table, each one depicting a channel marker. Luc's sister had known her craft. Each drawing was incredibly detailed, each channel marker subtly different, with moss growing up the ancient wood and each one of the placards revealing a number: 151, 174, 179.

"How many of these did you say your father put up?"

Luc stared, his gaze troubled. "Thirty."

"Channel marker system only goes up to one fifty," Gideon muttered. "Going to take a bit to match this to their locations."

I couldn't make heads or tails of it. "Hell, those could be anywhere and you know it."

Whatever he was about to say was cut off by the tinkling bell over the door.

Mose William stood shivering in the door, his jacket and jeans so drenched I thought it was going to blend in with his black skin.

CATFISH IN THE CRADLE

"Mr. Trucker, I've got some weary kids ready for some hot meals… spotted your lights still on. Going to come back for the canoes."

Before Davis could protest, a line of shivering teenagers came in, looked like a church camp by their appearance. Their chaperone was one of those new youth pastors with half of his head shaved; came in last searching for service on his cell phone. "Still can't get a signal."

Davis gave me a long-suffering look before smiling at the young man. "Let me fire up the grill. Didn't expect any folks to be out, Mose."

Mose clasped his hands together. "Thank you, Davis. Didn't think we were going to be out there that long. I'll owe you one."

The kids filed past us, taking a wide birth around Luc and Gideon. The Cajun hoodoo man eyed each one darkly before going back to staring at the sketches.

"Hey, Grady."

"Mose," I said as warmly as I could under the circumstances, shaking the man's head. "Hell of a storm."

The tour guide nodded his head loose, drops shaking out of his white hair and onto his equally snowy beard. "Been out camping the past few days, right there where Oxbow meets Alligator Bayou. Never let up once, no sir."

Mose was a little older than me and had lived his life on the border of perpetual poverty. He didn't really seem to mind it though, an easy life on the lake being his only goal in life. Easier to live free when you don't want.

We'd fished a couple of times together. My pop would have turned circles if he had seen me fraternizing with a black man, but even when we were kids back in the seventies, we hadn't seen color.

Things were better on that front nowadays, no thanks to the backwoods holdouts who judged a man on how he looked rather than how he worked. Fucking idiots.

Mose glanced past me at Gideon and Luc, shaking hands with the young fishermen and squinting his eyes at Luc, who was ignoring him, snapping his finger when he finally realized who was standing in front of him. "Well hot damn, son. You're Jean Phillipe's boy, right?"

Luc looked up, startled, staring at the old tour guide with newfound respect. "You knew my dad?"

Mose smiled. "Most certainly did. Your pa made the best damn crawfish etouffee in the South."

They drifted off into old memories of the Robichaude clan before their deaths, Mose telling old anecdotes of Bastienne and Cyprien canoeing with him, his momma Felicite once kissing Mose on the cheek for showing his siblings the best fishing holes.

"Hell of a woman your momma, beautiful like a sunset."

Ain't going to lie: it hurt me something fierce, made me miss Renee and Sammie Jo and happier times.

Banished it from my mind. Had the next few years to drink and reminisce before I shuffled off the mortal coil. My grandson needed rescuing. I could wallow later.

"Man those were good times. I was awfully sad when I learnt what happened to them."

CATFISH IN THE CRADLE

Luc nodded his head. "Yeah." Nothing more needed to be said.

Wandered over and gripped his shoulder. The Cajun hoodoo man nodded gratefully and went back to examining the three pieces of sketch paper, no doubt wracking his brain for any clues that his sister might have left.

Mose wandered closer. "What are you working on… oh."

I looked up at him. Wasn't often Mose was surprised by anything on this lake. He'd been out on it more than anybody I knew.

"A lot of folks been scratching their heads at those old posts for years. I know your daddy put them up, Luc. Helped him on a few of them, in fact."

All of us looked sharply everything around us seemed to go quiet as Mose sighed. "Never could figure the reason why he went about—" He noticed our expressions.

"Do you know where these are?" I asked, reaching out to grip his arm.

Mose looked taken aback by how serious I was. Probably saw the look of grim worry in my eyes. "Sure I know where they are, made a map a few years back."

My grip on his arm tightened. "Show us."

It was maybe a five-minute drive to Mose' place. Davis stayed behind to serve the kids, putting Misty up in his back office to let her grieve in her own way.

Mose lived in a modest cabin that he had built years ago with his own two hands; a tin roof that thundered like mini drums under the rain. What passed as a driveway was nothing but a muddy path.

The water splashed as Mose ushered us inside. The man was old school, even older than me. Never did hook up to the utilities instead preferring to boil his own water, keep himself warm with a fire… he lived damn ruggedly.

It was cold and dark inside, and Mose disappeared into the blackness while the three of us stood in the doorway.

A candle lit in the blackness and Mose' face appeared like the grim reaper himself, his white hair and beard casting shadows that reminded me of a painted-on skull.

"I'll be stoking the fire; map's buried under one of these piles of junk."

The cabin was pretty sparse. An old green chair with a hole in one of the armrests, a moth eaten bed on a pair of ratty old bedframes that didn't match, stone foundation that lay bare beneath our feet and had probably been the only thing that Mose hadn't cobbled together in his home. A few handmade shelves held some books, fishing poles on hooks nailed into the walls, ancient stove and table.

Luc began searching the bookshelves as I helped Mose gather some firewood from the small iron rack next to the old stove. Soon a warm orange glow bounced off the small interior, the flames eagerly licking at the dry wood and providing a little more light.

Gideon and Luc had pulled out stacks of old newspaper clippings, journals, and any other knick knacks what looked like it could contain a map.

"Don't have a TV, so I tend to write a lot. Apologies for the chicken scratch," Mose said as he stretched his fingers toward the fire, letting the warmth flood through his skin and bring a little life back into them.

"You got some mystical thing you can do to find the map easy?"

Luc looked at me with the long-suffering look of someone who had been asked that same question one too many times and it wasn't funny on the first one. "Might be able to conjure something give time and the proper ingredients. Don't have them now though unless you're willing to swim back to Gideon's houseboat, Mr. Pope."

I let the smart aleck remark slide as I grabbed the nearest journal and began combing through it.

Mose had lived a storied life. Wrote about me a few times. Glad to see that he didn't have a low opinion of me. Didn't find a map though.

Probably half an hour passed in that dark hole before Gideon turned a page in a large scrapbook. "Think this is it."

All of us immediately stopped what we were doing to crowd around Gideon; Mose had lit a lantern that he sat next to the younger man on the table.

The map was an old rendering, at least a decade maybe more, newer divisions and houses around the lake not marked yet. Jotted black lines marked the channels and occasionally intersected with a red dot. Next to that dot written in black scrawl were numbers: 151, 152, 153, et cetera.

"Instincts are right on the money, Gideon." I muttered as Luc looked up at Mose.

"Sir, do you mind if we borrow this?"

Mose smiled. "Mr. Robichaude, as far as I'm concerned it belongs to you anyway. Owe your family a lot."

Luc nodded gratefully and carefully folded the map and put it away. Gideon's keys jangled in his pocket. "Think I'll go start the car."

Mose looked on, curious. "What did y'all say that you were needing this for?"

I patted the old man's shoulder. "Trust me on this one Mose: you don't want to know."

CHAPTER TWENTY-THREE

WE GEARED UP FOR COLD weather. Sure the humidity was climbing and creating fog banks, but if you've ever spent time under an April shower in the South then you know how fast it can go from pleasant to fuck all freezing.

Gideon volunteered the *Minute Mother* for our travel. Made sense really seeing as Luc's ingredients were on it along with a fine collection of fire arms.

"Think I'm going to sit this one out boys."

Couldn't believe the words I was hearing coming out of Davis Trucker's mouth.

The teenagers ate all around us, oblivious to the things in the lake. We had returned expecting him ready to arm up and cast off, but instead he looked each of us with an even gaze.

"I've patched you up, given all of you shelter, but I've seen enough war, death, and strange things to last a lifetime. If I go out there with you I'm not coming back." He sighed and ran a hand across his bald head. "I'm not doing that to Helen, I just can't…"

My temper reached a boiling point and I reached out, poking two hard fingers into his chest. "Coward. You're a fucking coward…" I hissed the words, all of my venom and anger in that whisper. "I thought more of you, Davis Trucker. Thought you were a man of courage—"

With speed that belied a man of his size, he wrapped a hand around my wrist, holding it firm, those deadpan eyes as hard as stone. "Never mistake me for a coward, Grady Pope. I have a life, a wife, and I've done what I can to help." He looked at Gideon, Luc, and me in turn. "Maybe if I was like the rest of you and didn't have people who relied on me, I'd help out. But as it is… I wish you all the best of luck."

He released my wrist and my anger roiled in my chest. I balled my fist, ready to make him pay, when Luc's hand lightly patted my shoulder.

"Mr. Trucker thank you for what you've done, sincerely. If I was you I'd be doing the same thing." Luc chuckled darkly. "Not sure that we all shouldn't, but I ask only this of you: that if we don't come back, you'll get as many people as you can to leave Uncertain in the rear view."

Davis nodded his head. "You've got my word on that."

"Good enough," Luc said, tipping a small finger in salute. "Thank you for all your help my friend."

Davis grunted. "Best of luck to you boys."

He at least gave us food to take with us when we hit the river. "Least I could do," he said, my ass...

My temper practically boiled the water as we waded out to the *Minute Mother*. The river was nearly up to the diner door now and we were still about thirty yards before we began swimming the rest of the way.

I was near wheezing when Gideon hauled me up the railing, Luc coming behind me. My throat still hadn't healed. Despite my bravado and a lifetime outdoors, I knew I was pushing my body to the limits.

"Grady, do you know how to drive a houseboat?" Luc asked when we had sequestered ourselves inside and out of the rain. I nodded.

"Good, then I'm going to ask you to drive while Gideon assists me with some things." He glanced apologetically at Gideon. "That is with your permission of course."

Gideon held up his hands. "Let him go ahead. As long as he's not plowing us into trees I guess it doesn't really matter."

"Where's the console at?"

Gideon pointed outside. "Under the awning right there. Can't miss it."

Luc quickly swept up Gideon, pointing out various ingredients that he had stowed around the interior that he needed for his conjuring. I let myself out quick. Could barely do math let alone whatever hoodoo he was cooking up. Maybe Luc had known that and asked that I go to the one place I knew that I could excel.

The houseboat console was a pretty plain thing. Chipped wood from too much time under the sun running up the sides, bits of black mold clinging to the steel levers, and pollen both old and new covered the buttons in a thin layer of yellow dust.

The awning was just good enough to keep the water out of my face, the beating rain echoing the continuous thumping of my heart. I reached out with a cupped hand, letting the cool liquid trickle in and tickle the pores of my skin.

After I had caught enough, I poured it over the console washing the pollen off and onto the green shag carpet. No use battling allergies along with the hypothermia I was no doubt acquiring.

Maybe this was the end of the road. Hell, I'd be happy if it was.

I keyed the ignition and the motor on the rear of the houseboat gurgled to life. Hauled up the anchors and cast off the mooring line. The current immediately began taking us, drifting slowly away from the receding shore and towards the big lake.

I swung us in a slow circle. Fucking thing was like handling a bus and I strained to keep us on a steady course.

Didn't feel completely at ease until I saw the channel marker. It was easy after that. We had quite a ways to go to get to our destination, a remote area on the northern side of the lake called Fishnet Gap.

Even when there's a flood some people just don't know when to quit. I had taken Government Ditch slow; couldn't afford to be knocking into the trees and putting holes in the hull before we had made it anywhere.

This unnatural flooding might have been a blessing in disguise. Normally I wouldn't have dared trying to take a houseboat down the channel. Fishing boats sure, but this giant whore wouldn't have made it to the first fork before bottoming out.

Still, the looks of surprise on the gator hunters faces brought a smile to my face.

Saw at least six boats, each of them stringing up drop lines baited with bloody entrails of various animals. Amateurs. Thought they could catch a gator by just baiting a hook with no regards to territory hunting patterns. They were out to make a quick buck rather than a living.

Prayed for their souls if the game wardens got ahold of them. I laughed a little at that sentiment; a man-eating alligator seemed so trivial now in comparison to what was beneath this lake.

In the end I just hoped that these men would make it off the river in one piece.

Left the more traveled routes behind once we hit alligator bayou. The fog made it slow going, and I kept my eyes peeled for each twist of the channel.

Gideon joined me on the deck, sliding the glass door behind him as he offered a small red pouch to me. "Luc says don't lose it this time."

Letting it drop around my neck, I grunted and nodded my head towards the glass door. Gideon's eyes followed me to Luc, still busy brewing god knows what. "Said that he didn't need me right now, that he needed to prepare for when we got there." Gideon shrugged. "Whatever the hell that means."

The both of us lapsed into silence as another turn in the river forced me to take a long arc to make it.

Gideon pulled a up a chair beside me and stared out at the gathering flood waters swiftly turning our home into a swamp. "Wonder when this will stop."

I laughed. "Never. It's going to be Noah thing, forty damn days and nights and then bam, its fish fucker all you can eat."

The younger man didn't share my mad laughter. "Been thinking about her... shot her cold...didn't even hesitate."

Whatever insane mirth I had gleaned was shot. "She betrayed you, tried to murder you, murdered Scott... can't fault her yourself for doing what you could."

Gideon pulled a small photo from his jacket pocket; it looked like it had been taken this past winter. Gideon and Vicky were huddled close together in the photo, happy and carefree, bundled up like a Hallmark movie.

"I know you loved her, but there's going to come another woman for you, hopefully one that's not shacking up with monsters."

Gideon ignored me and continued staring at the picture. He stood up and walked to the edge of the deck. The rain soaked him through quickly and he stood at the prow, staring at the brown waters.

Could have been crying when he flicked the picture away, the current dragging it under the boat and to the waiting propeller. I chose to believe it was the rain making me see things.

Neither of us said anything when he sat back down next to me.

We'd gone maybe another half a mile when the feeling started to nag at the back of my head.

Danger…

Close.

"Go inside and tell Luc to kill the lights."

I said it as calmly as I could, but Gideon could tell I was dead serious as he practically threw the chair overboard in his haste.

I didn't venture up this way much, so when Luc emerged asking me what was happening, I ignored him. "Get the map out. Any harbor big enough for this big bitch to hide in close by?"

Gideon flipped the chair up and Luc hastily spread the map out and began scanning the channels. "About a quarter mile up, there's a harbor off Kitchen Creek big enough to hold us… one-way in."

Gideon examined the map and shook his head. "I know this place. It's overrun with the salvinia. We go in we aren't getting out."

"No choice."

I could hear it over the sound of the rain, thundering boat motors moving much faster than us. Luc and Gideon heard it too by the time we reached the entrance to the harbor. I swung the boat starboard, the ancient wood groaning as I put it through its paces.

Even with the grey mist that hung over the lake I could see the swathe of green ahead of me. Looked almost strong enough to walk on. Prop began choking barely feet into the weeds, struggling to keep the propeller turning as the grass and mulch began clogging the blades. The salvinia closed behind us just as quick, flowing back into its place, covering our tracks easily.

With a shuddering cough the motor finally stalled out, and we came to a stop between the shoreline and the woods on the right and a copse of cypress trees on the left.

"Quiet now," I whispered and gripped the throttle hard. Didn't know who was coming up behind us but it didn't matter. Better safe than sorry.

The motors got loud, nice outboards in case they had to maneuver through the salvinia.

"Surprised we haven't caught up with them yet." Earl Ray wasn't even attempting hide his voice, arrogant ass.

"Folks saw them leaving in that eye sore Whyte calls a home. Bastard's going to pay for killing Vicky." Couldn't make out who else was with him. Hell, if I hadn't played poker with him every Saturday for five years I wouldn't have recognized Earl Ray's voice either.

Gideon tensed up next to me, tendons in his neck straining as he gritted his teeth together. Couldn't see them through the fog and rain, and if they hadn't been shouting at each other I wouldn't have been able to make out what they were saying.

"Think we should check out these bayous? Might have pulled in there."

"No way they could have heard us, rain's way too thick."

"I'm checking anyway. My prop won't clog up with that shit."

Luc hastily reached in his pockets producing a small candle and lighter. Never thought I'd see the day when Luc Robichaude didn't look confident, but his hand was practically trembling as he struggled to light the candle.

One of the distant motors got louder. Thought I could see the hint of a spotlight through the mist.

My hand lashed out and I gripped his arm hard. "They'll see the flame!"

"Trust me," Luc hissed back at me, the small flame licking at the wick and producing a nice warm glow. He began chanting prayers and incantations that I couldn't make out. The candle bled red wax that ran down the stem and onto Luc's hand, sizzling when it touched the skin. I saw my young friend wince, but he never stopped continuing to chant as his flesh scalded.

The motor was close now, definitely a searchlight scanning through the fog. I held my breath tight as my heart pounded in my chest.

"Don't waste the time. If Robichaude gets hold of them channel markers this whole thing is done. You aren't getting rich and neither am I."

The searchlight turned off, vanishing as a coughing backfire reached my ears. I breathed out a sigh as the motors and shouting voices growing more distant.

Luc immediately went to the edge of the boat and plunged his hand into the cool depths, the candle immediately hissing out. Luc grunting relief as he glanced back us. "It's a working to cloud men's minds. Usually do it in a candle holder though… hurt like hell."

Understatement of the year, and I found that I had newfound respect for the man; he had a pain threshold like none other.

"Why do they need to destroy them at all? Why haven't they just come to kill us?" I asked, curious.

"I expect it's because Lincoln is still fighting them. The mercury has done a number on them. Can't fight a holy war without your messiah."

A measure of pride pounded through my chest, Pope spirit at work: Don't give in.

"Religious fervor and degrading mental faculties don't mix well," Luc said as he squeezed his hand tight grimacing. "I can heal this but it's going to take time that we don't possess. Have any burn ointment on this tub?"

Gideon nodded his head back inside. "Right over where you've been working, actually."

I glanced over the side of the boat back towards the prop sitting dead in the water. "Best be arming yourselves too. Could use a little cover when I dive in to unclog the prop."

"Grady, I think I have a better chance and you've been pushing—"

"Get that burn cream on your hand, Robichaude, and let me worry about what I can and can't do." I wasn't going to have anybody pitying me or thinking I couldn't do something. I was old, not useless. The Cajun's lips thinned, and he followed Gideon inside without saying another word while I made my way around the side to the bow.

Double outboards. Couldn't tell how much shit had actually gotten clogged up in the works, and wasn't too optimistic about my chances of getting it clear either.

Couldn't reach the props from here, which meant a little trip below the water line. We weren't in any well-traveled path, which also meant alligators prowled. Irony at its finest that it would more likely be the animals that I had spent a lifetime hunting rather than a monster that finished me off.

Gideon and Luc both came out the back door holding twin rifles, .30-06 by the looks of them. If you wanted to keep a trophy those weren't the calibers to be going with. Now if you wanted to blow something away into the next county, then you were right on the money.

Gideon cocked the gun and began sweeping the water, Luc mirroring him.

None of us said anything. It was understood what could go wrong.

I eased myself into the water and my breath immediately caught in my chest. Damn chill went all the way down to my bones. I began feeling around the props, the triple plates of metal twisted up fierce with detritus. The salvinia had clogged them up good, wrapping tight around the shaft, hard bits of root really constricting around the blades.

"Either of you have a good knife?"

Gideon produced a blade from his pocket and I began the slow process of cutting through the vines, careful to keep a tight grip lest the tool go tumbling into the deep.

The chills racing up my spine had nothing to do with the temperature, and I went about my work as quickly as I could, the fear beginning to creep back into me.

I had made it through the roots wrapping around the second prop when I heard a distant boat motor and stiffened.

"Might want to hurry, Mr. Pope." Gideon said as calm as possible, steam coming off his brow.

"I'll check the prow," Luc said as he vanished into the mist. I redoubled my efforts, hacking at the roots as twin searchlights pierced through the fog.

"Y'all folks all right?"

The boat came to a stop next to us and I sighed in relief when I saw TEXAS GAME WARDEN emblazoned across the side. Larry Knowles and Desmond Miles leaned out wearily, bright neon raincoats shining under the flashing blue and red lights..

Desmond looked at Luc with wide eyes when he rounded the corner; Luc nodded his head. "Desmond, long time."

"Yeah, good to see you back, Robichaude."

I finished cutting the vines and crawled back out of the water, shivering as Gideon reappeared tossing me a warm blanket that I eagerly wrapped around myself. "What are you fellas doing so far out?"

"Looking for the assholes that are baiting their droplines with chicken. Don't have to explain to you how illegal that is."

CATFISH IN THE CRADLE

I glanced at Gideon, who mercifully didn't mention that I had tried baiting the man-eater with that exact same tactic. Might have known the gator was there, but illegal methods are still illegal.

"What are you guys doing so far out here? Taking on apprentices, Grady?"

Here came the moment of truth: if these men had been involved, they would have already been trying to blow my brains out. But as it stood I thought they could be trusted.

Would they believe us, though?

"Why don't you fellas follow us. Come on board; we don't have a lot of time, so we'll make it quick.

By the time we were done, Larry Knowles look at the three of us like we had lobsters crawling out of our ears. "Not wanting to insult you guys or anything, but you are aware of how completely insane this sounds."

Luc nodded. "Well aware of it but the facts don't lie, don't you think it odd that you haven't been able to find the Sheriff or Beau Caldwell?"

Larry shrugged "It's a flood things are crazy, power lines are down, these assholes out here on the river are trying there best to murder every poor gator they come across and you're talking some half ass redneck *Creature From the Black Lagoon* shit."

Yeah, this went about the way I expected it to. I gave a look to Luc before I gestured towards the door. "Thanks for taking the time to listen, but afraid we're going to have to cut this short. Can't let my grandson lead some sort of crusade against us if I can help it."

Larry Knowles looked like he wanted to haul me off and throw me in the nearest care facility. Didn't blame him for that; if Cy had still been alive and started talking about fish monsters living under the lake I would have readjusted his dosage as well.

"I believe them."

Desmond said it quietly, but he might as well have clapped his hands and done cartwheels. Larry looked like he was about to shit bricks.

"You can't be serious."

"Things I've seen, Larry, I'm willing to believe a lot… especially when a Robichaude is involved."

"All of that hoodoo crap was just that, just boogeyman shit meant to scare kids."

Desmond shook his head. "I believed that too, brother, but it's all real. You don't have to come but I'm going with them."

I nodded my thanks at him while Larry threw up his hands in exasperation, swearing as loud as he possibly could before pointing at the game warden boat attached to our hull.

"Well fine, let's get fucking going so we can play hero, dammit."

Gideon and Luc both expressed their thanks while I nodded in approval.

The two game wardens had returned to their boat when the splitting migraine almost caused me to topple off the side. Luc caught me as I doubled over. I heard distant shouting but couldn't make out what they were saying; my mind was a haze. The Cradle materialized in front of me.

This is the end, Grampa.

I heard Lincoln's voice in my head, drumbeats pounded heavily as a horde of deformed half-breeds jumped up and down, hollering mad obscenities in their alien tongue. Four of the primordial Deep Folk stood in the pool of mercury, clustered around the gigantic statues, their head bowed in supplication.

The biggest one, Vi'hocta, knelt at the monument's feet, repulsive tongue lashing out and lapping at the mercury oozing down the stone edifice. When he rose a deathly silence passed through the assembled horrors. My grandson's fear flooded through me along with other sensations that I didn't understand.

A hunger all consuming, my mind flashed with the memories of a million years and knowledge above my feeble understanding. I could see the workings of magic and the downfall of the Deep Folk from ancient wonders into primitive savages.

There was a thumping and the crowds parted way. The Deep Folk with the useless eyes made his way easily through the masses, sloshing into the pool of mercury, his whiskers twitching as it passed through the metal. Vi'hocta gestured, and Lincoln roared in defiance as they dragged him forward.

Impotent anger seized my heart. Wanted to reach out and strangle every one of the bastards. But it wasn't my body, wasn't my vision. I was just an observer... helpless.

Two eight-foot-tall Deep Folk dragged Lincoln to the edge of the liquid, and Vi'hocta reached out a webbed hand to his son.

Goodbye.

I raged helplessly as Lincoln walked into the tide pool. The masses began chanting, deep rhythmic croaks and warbles as the massive creature seized Lincoln's face, covering his eyes in darkness.

Then it plunged him down into the mercury.

Intense pride filled me as I felt my grandson struggle as long as he could to hold his breath When he finally gave in, I felt his mind deteriorate with each breath of poison. Couldn't remember his few days of life at first, then his name, then me, just a jumble of images and instincts.

When he was pulled back up to the surface, he looked around in confusion for a moment before roaring a challenge at anyone who would defy him.

None did.

He turned and bowed to his father, recognizing the alpha of the tribe… for now.

His father croaked, pleased with himself and handed him a spear.

Before the vision ended, I felt the rage beating in my grandson's chest and saw the discarded remains of human skin. No more humanity.

The sightless Deep Folk croaked. A procession of half-breeds came forth, their shuffling steps and arms straining to hold the body they carried.

CATFISH IN THE CRADLE

I saw my daughter, bloated from her time beneath the waves; could smell the stench of rot around her. They laid her body at Lincoln's feet and I felt his indifference. There was nothing in his heart for this dead surface woman, only hunger.

He reached down with his hand, the fused flesh wrapping easily around his mother's dead face. He tugged, and the skin came free easily, bits of bloody and putrid tendons hanging free. He clutched my daughter's face in his hand like a rag. I got to stare into her dangling eyes as he brought it to his mouth and chewed; could taste the rot in my own.

The Deep Folk croaked out cheers of joy and joined my grandson in the mercury pool, all of them eager to join in the meal.

I was weeping when Luc's face came back into frame, the others crowded around him.

"Saw him… saw him down there."

Luc didn't need to ask as he clutched the mojo bag around his neck and whispered prayers.

"Maybe he can buy us some time."

I looked at Gideon, stifling my tears and retreating to that primitive part of me that held my rage. "No. They're ready, and they'll be coming soon. He ain't human anymore."

CHAPTER TWENTY-FOUR

GIDEON TOOK THE HELM WHILE I recovered. I appreciated him for that and for the others leaving me be while I worked through my despair. I was truly alone in the world now; the bastards had forced it out of him, everything that connected him to this world.

Swore I would kill them all, give them pain like they had never experienced. With the remainder of my time on this earth, I would make them pay. And aAt this rate that wasn't going to be a long time and I didn't give a damn.

What was left anyway?

My daughter's severed face hung in my mind as I raised myself off the couch. I'd felt Lincoln's instincts... what his father had told him. The surface dwellers had betrayed them, had poisoned their seed and forced them to live in the Cradle. Their god had sent signs, promises and omens that the half-breeds would be redeemed. Lincoln had been that sign, and once the Robichaude markers were gone, nothing would stop them from retaking the surface.

Monsters wouldn't know what hit them once they were done killing everybody in reach. I'd reckon that the government would come in and do a little sweep and clear or maybe just sterilize the whole lake to be safe.

I chuckled to myself; maybe it would be better that way.

Luc figured that they would have already found the nearest channel marker at the end of Kitchen Creek. The two game wardens took point and guided us around Potter's Pass, heading back towards Government Ditch and more civilized areas.

I wiped the tears from my face and joined Luc and Gideon on deck, checking the gun cabinet before I went and selected a nice ten gauge shotgun. The gun could dislocate the shoulder of a two-hundred-pound man if held wrong, but I wasn't taking any chances.

Neither of my companions said anything; just nodded.

"We're close maybe a few hundred yards. Luc whispered.

The rain had stopped; Luc took it as a bad omen. "They've swollen the river enough to get in easy reach of the houses. No use maintaining a working that powerful."

The motors rumbled through the eerie stillness. The mist remained to cover the world, but without the rain I felt naked outside, the shadow of every tree in the fog a monster ready to strike.

"Should be around here," Gideon whispered staring down at the map and throttling back on the motor.

CATFISH IN THE CRADLE

"Think we found it!" Larry hollered, earning him an urgent whisper from Luc who gripped the deck rail something fierce.

"Quiet yourself."

The two game wardens were close enough that I could see the look of distaste cross Larry Knowles face before Desmond put a warning hand on his partner's shoulder. He calmed down.

The channel marker hung slightly askew close to the river bank. Placard on the side was 171.

Had to hand it to the late Jean Phillipe; his craftsmanship had been superb. The carvings and runes, while both alien and terrifying, had a flowing beauty to them, unmarred by graffiti or vandalism of any kind. Couldn't help but admire it. Never had been a fan of art but this thing evoked feelings of awe.

The cypress moss hung around it like a veil. The salvinia present near the rest of the bank didn't dare creep further. Whatever power was in this thing keeping it free of any muck.

"Can we tie off to it?" Gideon asked. Luc nodding in return. I helped tie us off while Luc disappeared inside, Desmond and Larry anchored close by scanning the water for anything out of the ordinary.

Even after a heavy rain and the fog there should have been more noise: frogs, distant alligators, and at the very least a few birds.

Instead there was the silence.

Luc reappeared, carrying a satchel that he had no doubt pilfered from Gideon's closet. "Catch!" He lobbed a pair of red mojo bags over to Desmond and Larry. "Put them on, and when the shit really hits the fan clutch them tight and recited the Lord's Prayer."

Neither of them protested, to their credit. Maybe like me they just went along with the madness. Larry rolled his eyes but did as he was told.

Luc sat three candle holders at equal distance in front of him and on both sides. "Grady, would you mind?" I stepped forward and he handed me the candles, passing his rifle off to Gideon before sitting cross legged in a circle.

Each candle had been carved. My eyesight was still recovering and I had to squint, but I reckoned that each one looked like a miniature version of the channel marker in front of us.

"Sympathetic totems," Luc muttered, seeing my confusion. "Helps me work through all three of them over distance." He sighed as I placed each one in the holders, lighter in hand. "They'll be coming once I start this, and once I do, there isn't any interruption if we want this to work."

I lit the first candle. "How exactly is this going to work?"

Luc smiled a devil's grin. "Never explain the magic, Grady Pope, or else the magic goes away."

There was a rumbling in the air when I lit the last candle, a peal of thunder that echoed across the lake. Luc began chanting, words in languages I couldn't grasp echoing on the air.

"You boys best be ready. It's happening now."

Desmond heeded Gideon's words, cocking his rifle and scanning the water diligently while Larry lounged against the console.

The sound of boat motors came drifting through the fog, still far out yet but getting closer.

"I'll take the top." I nodded at Gideon as he climbed the ladder to the roof of the boat, laying down flat and aiming his rifle towards the fork off our starboard bow.

Nothing had appeared yet, but the whoever was out there throttled back on their motors. If it was the members of the cult, they were running silent now, probably worried that we were close by and would be able to hear them coming.

Three speed boats and a party barge emerged from the mist, each one crewed by three or four people who shouted in alarm when they saw the *Minute Mother*.

I cocked my rifle and waited. Earl Ray's voice came drifting across the channel. "Grady Pope, I know you're over there. Give us the Cajun and we won't be causing you boys any harm!"

"*Get fucked!*" I yelled back at him as loud as I could.

Desmond reached out and flicked on the matching red and blue sirens that bathed the mist in the duel colors. "Now you boys need to calm down. We don't take threats like that lying down."

I could see my former friend on the deck of the party barge, a rifle held at his hip while the rest of the men aimed at us warily. All of them looked sick, like they had eaten something that disagreed with them. Miss Franklin, Nate

Biers, Sue Ray, people I had known for years ready to murder us for greed.

"This ain't either of you fellas' business. Best motor on out of here before you both see something that'll give you nightmares the rest of your life…"

Neither game warden moved, both of them sweeping across the crowd warily.

"We don't want to harm y'all, but we're under a time clock. They need Robichaude dead… help out and there might be a little something in it—"

A long dulcet tone echoed through the trees and mist, loud enough to drown out Luc's chanting.

I'd heard that deformed sound before, and my grandson pushing his thoughts on me had provided understanding.

It was a war horn.

They were here.

Earl Ray's barge rocked as something massive passed beneath it, creating a wake and sending the men grasping for leverage. One bastard wasn't fortunate and went tumbling off the side.

A Primordial Deep Folk, all ten feet of tooth and scale, erupted from the water and caught the unfortunate man in its jaws like a massive bass taking a water bug. A bright red splash of blood as the guillotine teeth came down on the man's torso. His keening wail of agony reached a crescendo, ribs poking through his chest as his throat filled with blood. The Deep Folk reached up and with a twist ripped the gurgling head of the man from his neck, splattering the boat underneath with gore. Most of them screamed and fell to their knees, averting their eyes as their master revealed itself in its terrible glory.

Larry stared in abject horror at the thing scant feet away from him while Desmond looked grim.

Another one rose from the deep, and another.

Vi'hocta himself rose last, towering above the others, fifteen feet of muscle and scale. Dark eyes scoured the assembled boats, mouth opening in sucking gasps.

Drumbeats and bellowing horns echoed through the woods as the deformed children came shambling through the brush and bobbed to the surface of the water. Savant Huber, arm hanging askew, his bloated face split with a grin of triumph, hobbled at the forefront, vestigial gills uselessly tried to breathe as he spit a warbling hiss in our direction.

"*Grrraaddddyyyy.*"

Dozens of them lined the shore, each of them clad in rags or nothing, malformed genitals swinging each way as a few made crude gestures at us.

Then there was a mighty roar, and a fifth primordial Deep Folk rose from the water. It was smaller than the rest, barely gracing seven feet, but its foul hide didn't bear the story of scars and ritual marks the others did.

I knew my grandson when I saw him.

Smaller Deep Folk appeared out of the water, the ones who were direct descendants from their primordial sires, and even they displayed deformities. The warbling croaks and growls echoed all around us, overlying Luc's chanting.

There wasn't going to be a fight; it was going to be a fucking slaughter.

Larry clawed at his eyes, mewling obscenities; Desmond gritted his teeth but never let go of his weapon. Good kid. If we survived this, I was sure going to see we had a beer at Johnson's Ranch.

The cultists bowed as Lincoln approached them. The five primordial monsters backed away letting their messiah approach.

"My lord we are your humble—"

Earl Ray didn't have time to whore himself out any further before my grandson stabbed the spear he carried through the man's chest. Bits of heart and bone exploded out of his back while Lincoln reached a webbed hand inside him and pulled the man's entrails out in a steaming pile. In a swift motion he pulled the spear free and tossed the silently gasping man into the waiting maws of his compatriots, who tore into the flesh with wild abandon.

Bits of blood and sinew flew everywhere, and I saw Larry collapse to the deck, vomiting. The cultists began screaming as the gigantic fishmen tore into their flesh, desperate gunshots giving way to agonized screams.

The message was clear: we don't need you anymore.

I didn't feel pity as I watched these men and women die badly. Teap what you sow and all that. Did feel fear though, fear about what these things would do after they had devoured their erstwhile followers.

Didn't have to wait long.

One of the candles had burned quick, the wax pooling at the bottom of the holder.

CATFISH IN THE CRADLE

Lincoln turned around and gestured towards us with the spear, pressing a horn that had been carved from ancient oak to his lips and blowing a long, mournful tone.

The half-breeds charged forward, and I fired the ten-gauge directly into the first one to hit the water. The thing's putrid chest exploded as the buckshot tore out its insides. It dropped to its knees, mouth opening and closing before a few of its fellows brought it to the ground and proceeded to devour it.

I heard a shot behind me; one of the ten-foot monsters roared in pain clutching its eye, a useless pulp of black muscle and blood running down its face.

Ducking a chunked spear and firing in return, I grinned as a half-breed's good arm was torn off in bloody shards of bone and scale.

Larry screamed and fell on his back, scrambling to get away. He fired his rifle and the shot went wide, failing to hit any of the half-breeds hopping onto his boat, rocking the vessel and causing Desmond to lose his balance. Larry desperately tried working the bolt on his rifle, the half-breeds stalking closer.

One of the primordial ten-footers ducked through the water and rushed forward, flippers propelling it like a missile underwater, rising in wrath and hoisting the boat onto its side, sending its own spawn toppling into the river. Desmond lashed out and grabbed a railing just in time holding himself steady as Larry went sliding off into the water.

The Deep Folk swarmed like piranhas; the game warden floundered to the surface, struggling to reach for the mojo bag around his neck.

Poor bastard never had a chance as one of the water-bound monsters thrust a spear into his chest and began twisting. Larry's agonized wail reached my ears as his insides were torn from their places, bones widening and cracking in explosions of marrow. The monster hoisted him out of the water, rotating him on the spear like a pig on a spit as its smaller kin leapt from the murk and took great heaving bites from his flesh. A leg severed at the ankle, then the knee, a chunk of his side exposing bleeding organs and shattered bone.

When his wail quieted to dying gasps, the monster dropped him back in the water, the rest of his body becoming an easy meal for its compatriots.

The half-breeds had made it to the boat, climbing the hull close to Luc; I pumped shot after shot, killing a few and injuring others. A few dove back into the river to avoid my shots.

Savant Huber glanced at the hoodoo man and his candles… two had burned down.

I hadn't been counting my shots; didn't know if I had another in the chamber or not, but neither did the mockery of a man standing in front of me.

"You can't… stop us…" His croaking voice caused my stomach to roil, and I aimed the shotgun at his face oblivious to the sounds of slaughter all around me.

Huber's mouth plopped open in a wet gurgling roar and he rushed the hoodoo man. I pulled the trigger, praying, and was rewarded by the bark of the gun and Savant's head exploded in a shower of brain matter and bone. He fell twitching to the deck as the spent shell fell smoking onto the ruined carpet.

There was a splashing sound and I turned to find Lincoln stepping easily out of the water onto the deck, gesturing with his spear, half-breeds following in his wake.

The game warden boat capsized, and I saw Desmond dragged beneath the waves.

I let my rifle drop limp at my side. Gideon was still firing, but we had lost. Never knew that we could have won in the first place.

Out of ammo and out of time, I clutched the mojo bag around my neck. "Do what you have to do, boy."

Lincoln warbled a war cry and took three giant leaps, wrapping his hands around my neck.

Thought my neck was about to break; couldn't breathe. My fists pounded against my grandson's flesh; might as well have been punching iron.

My vision was turning red and my lungs burned.

"Our father... who art in heaven..." I gasped out.

There was a crack of thunder and Lincoln dropped me like a stone, screeching as he fell back.

The Mojo bag around my hand burned against my neck.

Think my opinion of magic was turning around.

Didn't have much time to recover as a shadow loomed over me and I turned, aiming as Vi'hocta's hand closed around my waist and lifted me into the air.

Heard Gideon scream, but I couldn't see him, twisting in the wet grip as hard as iron.

My eyes hurt to see the beast this close and twin streams of blood erupted from my tear ducts as Vi'hocta screamed something at me in its warbling tongue.

Couldn't understand a word but the message was clear: *I'm fed up with your shit.*

Barely had time to gasp out "Our—" before he started squeezing. The air exploded out of my lungs and all I could do was gasp and say my goodbyes. Hoped Luc and Gideon could finish what we had started. Had done my best, put the hurt on.

Was looking forward to death.

I was practically unconscious when I heard the roar of pain. It cut through the blackness like a scalpel.

Pain shot up my entire body as I hit the deck; pretty sure I cracked a few ribs.

Vision was hazy, but I saw almost black blood tinged with silver pumping out of Vi'hocta's leg from the spear jutting from it.

Lincoln stood defiant, his back close to Luc's own.

"Gram... pa..."

Good boy.

Vi'hocta roared in defiance and shuffled forward.

The last candlewick extinguished as a rumble peeled the air. Luc finished chanting and stood facing the monster, unafraid. "That's quite enough of that."

The half-breeds immediately began gasping for air as they clawed at their necks. Most of them that were still on the shore or on the boats toppled back into the water. The small Deep Folk immediately dove, and the four primordial monsters screamed incoherently as they pawed at their gills, raking bloody lines down their own flesh.

Lincoln's thoughts drifted into mine, a little magic going a long way. Luc had poisoned the air. It burned them, and it was burning him now.

Vi'hocta still stood on the deck, grasping at his gills as great gouts of blood erupted with every breath and ran down to the deck. He reached for Lincoln, who dove off into the water. Luc strode purposefully toward the fifteen-foot monstrosity, his hands twisting in ways I didn't understand.

Vi'hocta swiped at the Cajun hoodoo man. The monster was slow, sluggish; Luc easily avoided the swipe and stabbed an iron nail into its webbed hand.

Wanted to move, wanted to help my friend, but I could barely breathe and every twinge of muscle brought fresh agonies.

Had to give the old monster credit. He was literally bleeding from the neck but took the time to remove the iron nail and drop it to the deck before going on the attack again.

Gideon fired into the thing's shoulder; he was bleeding profusely from five talon marks across his belly, deep enough that I could practically see his stomach. His skin was pale as ice, hands moving clumsily, struggling to reload and fire another round as Vi'hocta staggered towards him, each step punching holes through the *Minute Mother's* deck.

Luc avoided the sweeping tail and scrambled for the iron nail rolling across the deck towards the water.

Gideon fired the bullet, barely piercing the monster's chest, collapsing on his back as he clumsily attempted to avoid the monster's retaliation.

The monster looked like it was on its last legs. The blood was spilling out of its gills fast and every step was taken with a stagger. Its fist rose in the air and Gideon raised his rifle in a vain attempt to save himself.

The balled flesh of muscle and claw broke the rifle like it was a twig and smashed into Gideon. He gave out a gurgling cry… died instantly as his ribs shattered and his organs were pounded to a pulp. The monster didn't stop as it gave out a warbling hiss and continued mashing the dead man over and over again.

We were sinking. I saw water begging to pool on the deck as we listed to the side. Luc was scrambling, looking everywhere for the nail that Vi'hocta had pulled form his hand.

It was rolling towards me.

Gritting my teeth and hauling myself to a sitting position, I reached out and grabbed it, gasping out Luc's name as he hastily snatched it from my grasp. The hoodoo man reached into his pocket and produced a mojo bag staring at the monster's back as it finished off Gideon.

"Just as I have pierced your hand, I pierce your heart."

He drove the nail through the mojo bag and the gigantic Deep Folk groaned and stiffened, his warbling gasps silencing. Its hands went to its chest and it clawed over its heart. A dark smudge spread beneath the scales and bits of mercury and blood ran out from the cracks. A long wailing moan erupted from its throat along with a torrent of bright red blood that splashed across the deck, Luc worked the nail deeper.

CATFISH IN THE CRADLE

The primordial Deep Folk chieftain fell with a groan, crashing through the houseboat's living quarters like a falling tree and lying still with a pitiful groan.

I grinned in victory. We'd won... I couldn't believe it.

Luc sank to his knees with a groan, lying against the deck even as the bow slipped beneath the water.

"Gotta get out of here, Grady..."

Lincoln appeared, standing waist deep in the water next to me; blood was beginning to leak out of his gills as he took shallow agonized breaths.

He reached out and placed his gnarled webbed hand on my chest.

"Grampa... I'm... sorry."

His voice was like a rumbling wave, and each word sounded unnatural coming off his tongue. I didn't think he would be speaking much English out of that monstrous mouth for much longer. He didn't look remotely human anymore, but his eyes, those dark pupils displayed an understanding... memories.

"Why?" I croaked out.

Luc crawled across the deck and flopped next to us in his exhaustion "Your mojo bag... when you called the magic it knocked some things about in his head."

The Cajun man smiled at Lincoln. "Brought some memories back up, didn't it?"

He tried to return the smile, his mouth twitching as he tried to form an expression it wasn't capable of making.

"The spell will wear off eventually; just like the fog is going to come rumbling back into your mind... you have to keep the bastards down there until I'm done, Lincoln."

My grandson grasped at his gills, each one bleeding heavily "Can't... stay..."

I felt fresh tears at my eyes, and they had nothing to do from pain.

Luc shook his head. "By the time what they've done to you comes rolling back, you won't remember you wanted to, just like they won't remember your help in killing..." The three of us glanced at the massive corpse behind us.

"Can you do that for us, Lincoln?"

The double eyelids blinked, then he nodded.

Luc nodded as well. "Good, then I'll get to my working."

Maybe he knew that I wanted to tell him goodbye, maybe he told the truth... either way he rose and left me with my grandson at the edge of the boat separated by railing and water.

"I love you, boy."

I said it suddenly. Wasn't sure if I even meant it, but it was out there all the same. I'd known him for a week and seen him transform from a babe to a man to a monster.

He was still my blood.

The webbed hand grasped mine and made my skin roil. "Take... care... of..."

His lips couldn't form the last word and I saw his face twist in rage before he released me and dived back under the water.

Barely left a ripple on the surface.

CHAPTER TWENTY-FIVE

WHATEVER MAGIC LUC WORKED DIDN'T have any immediate effect. Told me that he had sealed the entrances to the Cradle and that he was sure the Deep Folk were trapped beneath the lake for good.

Had my doubts on that; how could he be sure that he had gotten them all? Chock it up to magic hadn't made much sense to me before, so I didn't expect it to begin now.

We found Desmond washed up on the shore. Poor boy had been mangled beyond all belief. His face had a mess of gashes running across them. One of his eyes dangled uselessly from its socket and he was missing arm at the elbow. Besides that he was mostly intact and to my shock was breathing.

We hauled him out of the water, no easy task considering my cracked ribs and every breath was like agony.

Luc waded back out to the wreck of the game warden ship and began fishing around underneath for the radio. Put out a call for help, and was still doing at it when my age caught up with me and I passed out.

Woke up in the hospital. Could barely see anything and when I did get answers they were always things like, "We'll know more after we run a few tests."

Apparently, the diagnosis wasn't all too great.

Mercury poisoning, advanced.

Didn't have to tell them where I thought I had gotten it from Didn't want to think back to those memories.

Desmond recovered as far as Luc told me. Mangled for sure, but Davis offered him a job down at Shady Glade in lieu of his continued work at the Fish and Wildlife office.

And he told me that it was just a matter of weeks until I was going to go bugshit and begin seeing things.

If I told them what had been happening the past few days, I'm sure they would have thought that it had already begun.

Hell, how was I to know it hadn't?

Luc checked me out of the hospital. They had recommended me go to an old folks' home until the end, but I told them to shove their own dicks where the sun didn't shine. The hoodoo man promised to take care of me until the time came.

I'd been in the hospital for about a week but apparently there had been nary a peep from the Deep Folk. I didn't think much of it… the thought of my last kin trapped down beneath the lake in that den of monsters didn't fill me with happy thoughts.

By the fifth day at home I couldn't walk anymore. My muscles just couldn't lift me out of my chair. Luc came down and helped me shit, helped me eat, helped me do just about everything that needed to be done.

Misty Carter, Davis and Helen, Desmond, old Mose William… all of them skirted in and out of the house, none of them speaking much and just shooting the shit like I wasn't dying, like the river hadn't flood, like monsters didn't exist…

Had been home for two weeks and I was starting to pray for death. Could barely speak a fucking sentence now and I can't feel my hands and feet.

Death was coming. Breathing was beginning to become a pain in the ass. Had been seeing Renee too.

Told Luc just to take whatever he wanted, sell the house and make some money. Wrote it down with what little strength I had left. Good riddance: I was tired of looking at all of this.

Not that there was much money to be had. The flood had washed up inside and ruined a good bit of the house and what little possessions I had.

Luc left me out on my back porch in a rocking chair so I could look at the river and feel the breeze on my face with a good breakfast of eggs and bacon.

It was a good clear day, not a cloud in the sky.

Watching the river run was about the only thing that brought me peace these days. mesmerized me and kept the voices and Renee from saying much too me until I fell back into a nice sleep.

Luc had run back up to his house to get some things. Apparently magic can do a lot, but healing requires ingredients and sacrifices we didn't possess and weren't willing to make.

Still, he was trying to soothe me the best way he could. Couldn't hold that against him.

A dead alligator bubbled to the surface, its glassy eyes staring at nothing, belly slit from neck to groin and its insides hollowed out.

Fifteen-footer if I had ever laid my eyes on one. I knew it was the one that I had hunted just a scant three weeks ago.

A solitary member of the Deep Folk appeared out of the river, dripping wet and carrying a wicked looking trident, the serrated metal tips of the weapon undoubtedly built from sunken boat hulls.

Luc had said that the spell would wear off but had also been confident in his sealing of the Cradle entrances.

Damn arrogant boy.

The monster hauled the alligator behind him, dragging the massive carcass as easily as a toy wagon.

I knew it was Lincoln, knew there wasn't a mind left in that head just savagery. Seven feet tall with no deformities, my grandson had become quite the specimen, he'd already ritually scarred himself, the fishing hooks piercing his skin in various places, lures hanging off of them like symbols of victory.

CATFISH IN THE CRADLE

Wasn't going to beg or plead. The trident piercing my gut was going to feel like sweet release next to the hell I'd been living in.

I fixed my grandson with a withering gaze as he dropped the carcass next to me, planting the trident, and grinning wickedly.

His teeth were sharp. A tattoo had been applied to his face, symbol I didn't recognize.

He opened his mouth to speak and his voice came out in a sharp croaking rasp.

"Take… care… of… you!"

He gripped me with a massive hand and hauled me out of the chair. I slapped at that massively muscled arm.

Terror filled my chest as I gurgled a cry for help that came out as bubbling slobber. He opened the alligator carcass and with a last gurgling cry he stuffed me into the rancid reptilian darkness.

Felt him lift the body and I jostled around, trying to breathe.

Didn't begin screaming until I felt the water splash inside.

WILE E. YOUNG is from Texas, where he grew up surrounded by stories of ghosts and monsters. During his writing career he has managed to both have a price put on his head and publish his southern themed horror stories. He obtained his bachelor's degree in History, which provided no advantage or benefit during his years as an aviation specialist and I.T. guru.

Made in the USA
Columbia, SC
09 September 2024